❈❈❈❈

"Crayfish! There's our breakfast!" Jasper leapt into the water. It wriggled out of his grasp and beat a panic-stricken retreat towards a hollow in the bank.

"Jasper!" yelled Rosemary, pointing to the creature. The crayfish was undergoing the most amazing changes. It scrabbled frantically to push itself into a hole which was much too small, but the head which butted against the bank was human one minute, crayfish the next. Then a claw would change into a hand, and back.

Jasper crept up behind and hauled it out of the water and said, "Whichever you are, fish or human, make up your mind so we can talk to you!"

The crayfish became a very small boy, who opened his mouth, screwed up his eyes, and shrieked with terror.

"Don' cook me on the fire! *Please* don' cook me!"

"Of course not! We don't eat little boys."

"Oh." The child stuck a thumb in his mouth, around which suddenly sprouted a set of whiskers like a seal's, and stared at them.

❈❈❈❈

LORNA BAXTER
THE EGGCHILD

ILLUSTRATIONS BY
CHARLES VESS

ACE FANTASY BOOKS
NEW YORK

THE EGGCHILD

An Ace Fantasy Book / published by arrangement with
E.P. Dutton, Inc.

PRINTING HISTORY
E.P. Dutton edition / 1979
Ace Fantasy edition / December 1985

ISBN: 0-441-19258-0

Ace Fantasy Books are published by
The Berkley Publishing Group,
200 Madison Avenue, New York, New York 10016.
PRINTED IN THE UNITED STATES OF AMERICA

For my family, and Alison,
with many thanks

Contents

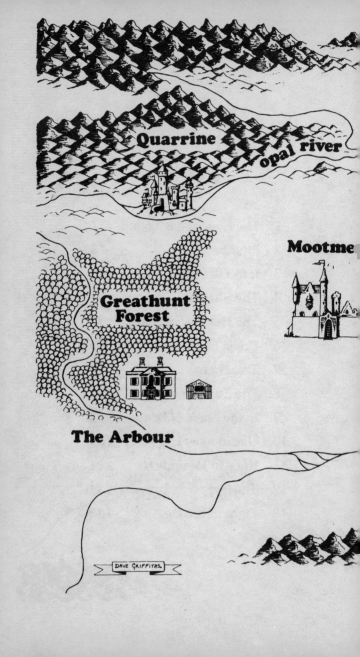

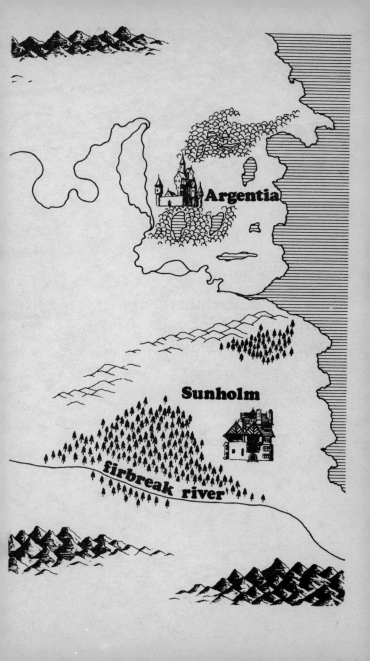

THE EGGCHILD

1

The Eggchild is Found

🔁

"Rosemary!"

"Shh!"

Rosemary frowned as she climbed the rickety ladder to the hayloft. She didn't speak until she'd closed the trapdoor behind her.

"D'you *want* someone to find you? Is it *you* singing, Jasper, and what's that light? You know Corrie told you you couldn't have a lantern up here because of the hay. You might start a fire . . ."

The boy put a hand firmly across Rosemary's mouth, grinning as her green eyes glared at him.

"I know you're afraid I'll give myself away, but I won't, I promise you. I could tell by the footsteps below that it was you coming. Now, where's your brother?"

"Keeping watch at the stable doors in case the grooms come back from lunch. What *is* that light then?"

"That's what made me excited enough to call out. Come and see it."

Together, Rosemary and Jasper floundered

over the deep piles of hay, raising clouds of nose-tickling dust as they did so. At last, they both subsided in the dimmest corner of the loft, and stared at what lay half-buried in the hay there.

Rosemary gasped. "It's a child, a baby, isn't it?" Her voice tailed off uncertainly.

"Is it?" queried Jasper, in an odd tone, and Rosemary knew what he meant. When she had first looked, it had been a baby, a golden baby lying curled up in the hay, singing in a high, sweet voice to itself. Then, under their very eyes, it seemed to change, and what they saw was a many-faceted, strange-looking egg lying half-hidden under a mound of yellow-brown hay. Even as they watched, the baby was back again, still singing its strange song without ever moving its delicate lips. The golden light it gave off seemed to be a part of it, pulsating under the baby's skin, the egg's shell.

Very gently, Rosemary reached out to touch it, expecting it to be hot with all that light coming from it, but it wasn't. Its smoothness was somewhere between the fuzzy velvet of a baby's skin and the creaminess of an eggshell.

Jasper stared unseeingly at it.

"I'll tell you one thing," he said abruptly. "The way it got here was as odd as its looks."

It was Rosemary's turn to stare.

"D'you mean you saw who left it?"

"Not saw, no. Heard. Get Corrie up here, and I'll tell you both."

Rosemary didn't move, except to raise one hand, and make a curvy sign in the air. Jasper looked on with interest, and asked, "Is he coming?"

"Listen," said Rosemary, and, sure enough, they could hear light footfalls crossing the stable below, and then the creak of the ladder as Corrie climbed it. The trap-door squeaked open, and

Corrie's head appeared in the opening. He stared over towards them, and jumped to the same conclusion as Rosemary had.

"Put out that lantern, you idiots!" He skidded to a startled halt beside them, and gazed down at the Eggchild. His eyes wandered to Jasper and Rosemary, and then back to the golden child.

"What is it?" he whispered, and crouched down to stare.

"That's why we called you," said his sister tartly. "Jasper wouldn't tell me how it got here until you came to hear the story too."

"Hmmph!" grunted Corrie. "I wish you hadn't told the ivy to alert me, though. Ivy's one plant I don't get on with, and I almost yelped when it reached out a branch to tap me on the shoulder."

"Well, you tell me another plant that's growing close by where you were standing."

"You could always have fetched me yourself."

"Wake me up when you've finished squabbling," said Jasper, curling up in the hay. His two young cousins immediately went quiet, and begged him to tell his story. Jasper frowned, and lowered his voice.

"Well, late last night, when it was completely dark, and I'd been asleep up here for some time, I suddenly woke up with the feeling that I'd just heard a loud thump in the stables. The horses down below weren't moving, though, and then I heard a scuffling, sliding noise from *above* me, on the loft roof. I didn't know, then, that there's a trap-door in the roof as well as in the floor of this loft, but whoever, or whatever, was up there soon found it, and opened it. The sky was so dark that whatever came in was only a darker blot against the stars. It was big, and it was gasping like a man—and yet . . . I don't know. I'd almost swear it had wings, though I can't say why."

Jasper paused, with the Eggchild's golden light glowing on his craggy face.

"What did the thing do?" prompted Rosemary gently. There was something in Jasper's expression which told her he was really worried.

"That's just it! I'm not sure. At the time, I thought it just climbed down the winch-rope from the roof, and then back up, a few minutes later. Ah! *now* I remember!"

"What?" exclaimed Rosemary and Corrie.

"That's why I thought it had wings. It shut the trapdoor behind it, and I heard a bump and some clattering, and then the beating of huge wings fading into the distance."

"What a story!" said Corrie. "And you found —this—this morning, did you?"

"Only a few minutes ago. You see, I'd had such a scare that I didn't get to sleep for a while, and then I slept very late. I only woke up a little while before I heard Rosemary coming."

Corrie had evidently been thinking.

"I suppose we'd better take this thing to Madam-mother—"

"It's not a *thing*. It's an Eggchild."

Corrie looked as if he might start another argument, so Jasper cut in quickly, "D'you think she'll know what it is?"

"She knows a lot of things we don't yet. She'll know what to do."

"Ooh! I forgot. We got a messenger from Quarrine Castle this morning, asking Mother if she knew where you were, Jasper." The dimples in Rosemary's cheek and chin deepened as she laughed. "Your father's cross because you've gone wandering off again, and you can't be found on Quarrine territory. I think he's afraid you'll offend one of the other Families."

"What did your mother say?"

"She sent a message back saying she didn't know where you were, and could Lord John please advise her what to do about the plague of deer we've got here in the Arbour. They're eating all the crops as they grow!"

"That's bad," muttered Jasper. "If the crops in the Arbour fail, all the Four Families will go hungry, and their people with them."

Rosemary and Corrie nodded solemnly.

"Madam-mother's worried about a lot of things at the moment."

"Oh?"

"This plague of deer, ruining the whole territory of the Arbour since Father was killed. And there've been a lot of nasty-looking foreign strangers about, riding big black horses."

"Yes. We've had some of them over in Quarrine too, wanting to buy up the swords and weapons we make. Father calls them the Night Raiders, because when he refused to sell, they turned quite ugly, and he had to call the guards out from the castle. The men went away, but they came back and tried to raid the armouries at night. They didn't get away with anything," added Jasper with satisfaction. "It seems a bit mean to add to your mother's worries by taking her the Eggchild, but we can't leave it here."

"No. We'll take it in, and tell her we found it up here."

"Let me know what she says about it, and get me some food too, can you? I can't let Father go on worrying. If he got angry enough, he might cause an earthquake, and I'd hate that to happen. I'll have to go back to Quarrine tonight. I don't mind if you tell your mother I've been here once I've gone again."

"All right, Jasper. One of us'll bring some food before nightfall. It might be a bit difficult, though, because of Stan and Jem working with the horses.''

''Never mind. It wouldn't hurt me to go without food for a while, so don't worry if you can't get back. Hungry or full, I'll have done what I set out to do, and I'll be able to settle down again at home for a while.''

Corrie looked at his big cousin, and asked curiously, ''Jasper, what makes you go wandering? I mean, Rose and I don't have this need to go off and explore somewhere new. What does it feel like?''

Jasper grinned. ''Oh, it turns me pretty nasty for a while. I just start to feel irritable with my surroundings, and the feeling gets worse until I can't bear Quarrine Castle, and I've got to get out and away for a bit, to somewhere new and fresh.''

''I'm glad I'm not like that. But I think one reason why you wander is that each of the Four Families is supposed to stay on its own territory, so you know, every time you're crossing a boundary, that you could be letting yourself in for a beating when you get back or if you're caught!''

''Rose, you know me too well—What's that?''

All three froze, as they heard heavy footsteps below, and the friendly whicker of horses.

''Stan and Jem are back!'' whispered Corrie. ''Jasper, hide under the hay. Rose and I'll take the Eggchild in to Madam-mother, and see what she says. We'll try and come back before nightfall.''

Corrie wrapped the Eggchild in his light cloak, and picked it up. He shook hands with Jasper, and floundered away back to the trap-door. Rosemary flung her arms round the older boy and hugged him.

''It's been *nice* seeing you, Jasper. I'm glad you came. I expect Madam-mother'd be cross if she found out, though, so I don't think we'll tell her unless we have to."

"That's up to you and Corrie, Rose. It's been good seeing you too. Be sure to grow another inch by the time next Four-Family Council comes around. I don't expect I'll see you again before then."

Corrie was waiting at the top of the ladder, and he and his sister went down one behind the other, leaving Jasper in the darkness.

They walked through the stables, saying hello to the grooms, Jem and Stan, as they went past, then crossed the courtyard, and went into the main building of the manor. The servants' entrance they used led past the kitchens, along a corridor, and through a swing-door into the main hallway. Here they halted, and considered where they were most likely to find their mother.

"Library?"

"No." Corrie shook his head decisively, his straight, fair hair glinting in a shaft of light shining down the stairs. "Workroom," he suggested, and pointed upstairs. Rosemary agreed, and led the way.

Lady Fenella was seated near the window of her workroom, making lace, but she looked up as Corrie and Rosemary came in.

"May we see you a moment, Madam, or are you too busy?"

Lady Fenella gave one of her rare smiles to hear her son so polite and formal, but she nodded, and rose to her feet. She was a tall, graceful woman, with an air of no-nonsense about her. Her face was always sad nowadays, and none of the servants had heard her laugh since the day the huntsmen brought her husband home, so badly mauled by a wild bear that he died the next day. Corrie and Rosemary knew that she laughed with them sometimes in private, but it was very, very seldom.

The two children stepped quietly into the room, Corrie with his arms still firmly curved round the cloak-muffled Eggchild.

"Had a good morning, darlings?" asked Lady Fenella. Rosemary nodded, but didn't take her eyes off her brother, who was unwrapping his cloak. Immediately, the golden glow lit up the room, and Lady Fenella bent forward to look, asking, "Why, whatever is it? Is it singing?"

"We don't know what it is, and yes, it is singing," replied Rosemary.

Lady Fenella sat down with the Eggchild in her lap, and folded her arms around it protectively. Her eyebrows drew together in a puzzled frown.

"What*ever* can it be?" she wondered to herself. "One minute it's a baby, the next it's an egg!"

Corrie nodded.

"We called it the Eggchild, Ma'am, but where did it come from? Who does it belong to? I mean, do Eggchildren have parents?"

"That's a good name for it, Coriander, but as for your questions, I haven't any idea what the answers might be. Where did you find it?"

Corrie and Rose told about finding it in the hayloft above the stables, and Lady Fenella looked more and more mystified. It was only when she exclaimed, "But how did it get there in the first place?" that they realised there was a part of the story they couldn't tell without involving Jasper. They looked at each other guiltily, because they weren't used to hiding things from their mother. She didn't seem to have noticed anything odd in their silence, however, and she reached out to pick up a small silver bell from the table beside her. She rang it, saying, "I'll send somebody down to the village to find out whether there have been any strangers around in the last couple of days, who might have abandoned the child, Eggchild, I mean," she corrected herself as she looked down at the golden bundle in her lap.

There was a tap at the door, and Lady Fenella covered the Eggchild with a fold of Corrie's cloak again, before saying, "Come in. Oh, Marjorie, I'd like you to go down to the village, and ask whether there've been any strangers about during the last few days."

Apple-cheeked Marjorie bobbed a curtsey, and said, "Certainly, Ma'am. I'll go right away."

As soon as the door shut behind her, Rosemary asked, "What're we going to do with the Eggchild tonight, Mother?"

Lady Fenella lifted off the cloak again, folded it into a soft cushion, and laid the Eggchild on it before she answered. Her hands became busy with the lace bobbins as she thought.

"I wish I hadn't sent that messenger from Lord John straight back to Quarrine, this morning. He won't get there before tomorrow at the earliest, though, and I'm almost at my wits' end to know what to do about these blessed deer."

"I know. As soon as anything shows above ground level out in the fields, they nibble it off. They've already had all my winter green seedlings!"

"I'd noticed, Coriander. We'll have nothing, come winter-time."

"Why isn't there a family to look after the animals, like we look after the plants, trees and growing things . . ."

"And the Sards look after the stones, and the mines and quarries, and the metals and things?" Corrie interrupted his sister.

"I wonder *where* young Jasper is . . ." began Lady Fenella, then went on, "Princess Diana does look after all white animals, as well as night-time and moon weather, but old Sol of Sunholm just concerns himself with the sun and our day-time weather."

"But that's not the same at all!" exclaimed Rosemary.

"I know, darling. But it all works very well until we get a time like this, when things get out of hand simply because nobody can control the wild animals. People are being attacked by bears and wolves, the crops are eaten by deer; next thing we know, even the chickens, ducks and horses will start attacking us, let alone the crows and the bull! Now there are these strange, unfriendly men sailing off the coast of Argentia, and others trying to buy swords from Lord John. What *is* our country coming to?"

Corrie and Rosemary looked at each other in dismay. The angry-hurt look on their mother's face, and the furious speed at which she was flicking the lace bobbins, told them that she was thinking about Lord Peter Moschatel, their father, and wishing that he were there to help her. She wasn't looking at the children, so they did something they'd been practising for just such an occasion as this.

Rose stared hard into her brother's dark-blue eyes, and their four hands moved in slow, complicated movements in the air. A heady scent of hot summer roses and honeysuckle filled the room and, gradually, Lady Fenella's flying fingers slowed, and she put down the bobbins.

"Mmm. What a heavenly smell!" she sighed, breathing in deeply. "Your tutor's been teaching you well."

"Old Applepie Stumble never taught us that!" protested Corrie. "We found it out ourselves."

"Coriander! Your tutor's name is Mr. Appledore," said Lady Fenella sharply, but then she relented, and added, "If you worked that out between you, it was very well done. You must teach me the movements, too."

The children went pink with pleasure. For their mother to ask them to teach her something was a high compliment.

"What *are* we going to do with the Eggchild tonight?" asked Rosemary again.

Lady Fenella's eyes went far-away, and she said, "I'm sorry I ranted on just now, children. I suppose I'm having a feeling-helpless day. Never mind. Yes, the Eggchild. Well, I've a feeling Marjorie's going to come back and tell me there haven't been any strangers around recently, and if I'm right, I'm going to send the Eggchild straight to Lord John Sard. He can keep it safer in Quarrine than I can here, until we find out what it is, and where it came from. Until I decide whom to send it with, I think it would be safe enough in your bedroom in a doll's cot, Rosemary. I shan't be able to spare anyone to set off till tomorrow, anyway. You two should be with Mr. Appledore now, for afternoon lessons. Off you go. I'll let you know what Marjorie finds out."

The children kissed their mother and ran out, taking the Eggchild with them. They knew already that Marjorie had gone on a fruitless errand. Lady Fenella could ill spare a man to take the Eggchild to Quarrine, and Jasper was in the stable hayloft ready to set off home that very evening. And yet they couldn't see a way to arrange for him to take the Eggchild without giving him away.

2
First Escape

Rosemary went to bed early that night. She had had an active day, visiting Jasper in the morning, spending a long afternoon in the schoolroom with Mr. Appledore, and then making another visit to Jasper in the evening, to take him enough food to last him till Quarrine. Jasper laughed at the pack she had made up for him.

"There's enough here to get me to Argentia, let alone Quarrine," he chuckled, but Rosemary guessed that he'd eat it all before he got home. It was rarely that Jasper travelled straight from one point to another. He was forever making detours to investigate something that interested him.

None of them had been able to puzzle out a way for him to take the Eggchild to Quarrine without letting Lady Fenella know he was in the Arbour. The ruling was that each of the Four Families kept to its own lands. Lord John must have been embarrassed enough at having had to send a messenger to ask whether Lady Fenella knew where his son was, and if she had to write back saying Jasper

had been in the Arbour, all three of them would be in trouble with their parents.

"Best not say anything," said Corrie reluctantly, and they had agreed.

Now, Rosemary was thinking sleepily that Jasper would be waiting for moonrise before leaving for Quarrine. He had said that he could arrange to meet Lady Fenella's messenger as soon as he crossed into Quarrine, and take the Eggchild on to Lord John himself. That would save the messenger half the journey.

"Nice Jasper . . ." thought Rosemary, and drifted off to sleep, the Eggchild's song mingling with the shushing of the leaves of the clematis growing outside her bedroom window.

It seemed only minutes before she was awake again, and staring towards her open window. The gentle sound of the leaves had changed and now they rustled, "Danger, danger," in a raspy, urgent way.

Without moving, Rosemary slitted her eyes and peered through the dark, wondering why she felt that something that ought to be there was missing. No singing! That was it. There was not a sound from the Eggchild, only the rustlings, "Danger, danger, danger," from the leaves. The glow from the strange baby still lit the corner where she had laid it in a doll's cot . . . Rosemary's eyes swivelled to the window again. The leaves were shaking even more.

"Danger climb. Danger house. Danger," they hissed. And Rosemary acted promptly. Plants couldn't lie to a member of the Moschatel family. If a plant warned of danger, then there was danger.

She leapt out of bed, and ran to the window. Quietly, she thrust her head out of it, and looked down. Half-way between window and ground, climbing slowly but steadily up the thick clematis, was the dark bulk of a man. A slow, throbbing sound filled the air outside the house, and Rosemary began to feel terribly sleepy.

She pulled her head back inside, fighting off the sleepiness. Her fingers flickered through the air, and her mouth whispered strange words. The clematis stirred, and when Rosemary risked a look outside again, the climbing intruder was firmly caught about arms and legs, by thick whippy tendrils of the creeper. She nodded her satisfaction again, and shut the window, reeling muzzily as she did so.

As quickly as she could manage, she picked up the Eggchild, muffled it in a blanket to cover the glow, and opened her door a crack, ready to run along to her mother's room, and rouse her.

She whipped back at once, for coming slowly down the corridor towards her, looking inside each room as they came, were three more men, and the rising moon glinted on the drawn swords in their hands.

Rosemary thought fast. As soon as she had picked up the Eggchild, her mind had cleared miraculously.

What were the men looking for? They had passed Lady Fenella's and Corrie's rooms, and done nothing, and taken nothing. That left only one likelihood. They wanted something, and the something was at that moment silent and heavy in her arms.

Inspiration came to Rosemary as she heard firm, soft footfalls approaching her room. She couldn't hide, so . . . she rushed to her clothes-cupboard, and felt in the pocket of an old cloak hanging in there. Triumphantly, she pulled out a tiny metal pot, unscrewed the lid, picked up a pinch of the powder inside, and sprinkled it over the Eggchild. It disappeared. Another sprinkling, and Rosemary too disappeared.

The door opened quietly, and a sword gleamed evilly as a man stepped into the room. He turned to say something to his companions; the words were foreign, but the tone sounded disappointed. A second man pushed the first out of the way, came further into the room, and lit a candle. All the men were dressed from head to foot in black.

He doesn't expect to be disturbed, thought Rosemary. I wonder why Mother and Corrie don't wake up?

All three men were in the room by now, and she was afraid that one of them would bump into her. While they looked at her rumpled bed, and one of them opened the window, she started sidling towards the door. The man who had opened the window exclaimed loudly, and pointed down at the entrapped climber. The others rushed to the window, and Rosemary slipped through the door. Her bare feet made no sound as she ran down to her mother's room.

Lady Fenella went on sleeping deeply, even when Rosemary shook her. She tried Corrie next, with the same result, and by now she was beginning to feel cold. She gave up trying to wake him, and raided his cupboard instead. His feet were the same size as hers, and he was almost the same height as she, even though he was two years older. She took a warm cloak, a tunic, a thick sweater, trousers, and a pair of boots, pulled all except the boots on quickly, noticing how sleepy she became as soon as she let go of the Eggchild, re-sprinkled herself with powder from the pot, and crept downstairs.

Her one idea was to reach the hayloft, in the hope that Jasper hadn't left yet, and that he'd be awake. The sleepcharm might be confined to the house, and he would tell her what she should do now.

Rosemary flitted into the library, and over to the windows. She looked out and made sure there were no more strangers in sight before she opened one window, and dropped the short distance to the ground outside. From the corner of the wall by the library, a hedge ran all the way to the back of the stables, and she scurried along in its shelter. At the side of the stables was a small door, kept open day and night to allow a wanderer to spend a warm night in the hay. This was how Jasper had first got into the hayloft.

Cautiously, Rosemary eased herself into the stables, and her heart sank; every one of the horses was soundly, unnaturally asleep. But at least there was nobody to be seen. Watching where she put her feet down, so that the straw should not crackle if she could possibly help it, Rosemary crept across to the ladder, and hauled herself up it one-handed, Eggchild under one arm, and boots between her teeth.

The roof trap-door was open, showing that even the hayloft had been thoroughly searched, but it did serve to let in the light from the moon. Directly in the beams lay Jasper, fast asleep. The strangers had evidently found him, and pulled him out from under a mound of hay, but realising he was not what they wanted, they had left him where they had dragged him.

Rosemary put down the Eggchild to shake him, but felt so terribly sleepy after only a moment that she picked it up again. She sat and thought about escaping on her own, and had decided she could do it when there was a loud thump from below, and the sound of low, angry voices. She peered over the edge of the trap-door. Below in the stables stood six men, talking quickly to each other. She couldn't understand a word they were saying, but it was clear that they were very angry.

"I wonder if one of those men is the Eggchild's father?" she thought, but didn't believe it, because the Eggchild had stopped singing when they were near, as though it didn't want to be found.

She waited, then gasped aloud. The small sound was covered by the noise of six flints striking sparks from six tinderboxes. The sparks flew, and found ready firing in the hay lying about everywhere. Within seconds, the stables were ablaze, and the men ran out, laughing harshly.

Horrified, Rosemary wasted seconds panicking. She tried to drag Jasper towards the trap-door, but could hardly move him. He would roast alive! The Eggchild . . . maybe the Eggchild would wake him up. Quickly, she thrust the invisible bundle into Jasper's outflung hands. Fighting instant sleepiness, she counted a slow ten while she shut the trap-door in the roof, to restrict the flow of air to the fire below.

Swaying on her feet, she knelt to lay her hands on the Eggchild again, and felt her head clear. Keeping one hand on the Eggchild, she thumped Jasper urgently on the shoulder.

Jasper woke agonisingly slowly, but, as Rosemary continued to thump him, he rolled on his back, and muttered, "Must go home," then, suddenly wide awake, "What's that smell?"

"Smoke," coughed Rosemary from close beside him.

Jasper squinted through the darkness.

"Rose? Get out of here, quick!"

"Keep hold of the Eggchild," she ordered, thanking the Powers that Jasper didn't ask silly questions. "And keep your voice down. There's enemies about. I think they're your Night Raiders."

"What . . . ?" Jasper began, but Rosemary gave him such a shove in the direction of the trap-door that he almost fell through it. Seeing the fire, he realised for the first time the extent of their danger.

"You first," he ordered, and Rosemary scrambled down the ladder. The fire seemed to have roused the horses from their charmed sleep, and they were screaming and rearing in terror in their stalls.

Dodging the piles of flaming straw, Rosemary darted along the rows, opening each stall. The horses needed no encouragement. They bolted for the little side door, the fire turning their soft eyes blood-red.

Rosemary grabbed a bridle from the nearest rack, and held on to it as she stood in the door-way, waiting for Jasper. He came at last, swaying through the smoke. Forgetting for a moment that he couldn't see her, Rosemary grabbed him as he made to go out of the door past her, and hissed, "Where d'you think you're going? The men are watching out there, just in case anything beside horses comes out!"

Jasper stared wildly, his eyes bloodshot and streaming from the smoke.

"The smoke must've blinded me! Oh, Rose, what am I going to do!"

He sounded so utterly downcast that Rosemary could have cried in sympathy.

"You're *not* blind, Jasper. I'm invisible. I'm going to make you invisible too. Stand still."

She shook the last remaining grains of her powder over the boy, and he disappeared. Only just in time—with a hungry roar, flames shot up through the roof behind them, and the heat drove them stumbling forward. Rosemary managed to grab Jasper's cloak, and dragged him away from the manor, to which he had instinctively turned.

Keeping a picture in her mind of where they were in the grounds, she led away to the east, using every scrap of moonshadow to hide in, even though she was confident nothing could see them.

Finally, when she was sure that the Night Raiders had not even suspected that they had left the stables, let alone followed them, she halted in a small copse, half-way down the road from the manor to the village.

Jasper sat down heavily, and allowed something else to thump down beside him. Rosemary hoped it wasn't the Eggchild he had bumped like that.

When Jasper spoke, it was in an exasperated, gravelly tone.

"Now, young Rosemary, suppose you tell me what all this is about? First of all, how've we become invisible?"

Rosemary felt that he must be able to see the crimson glow from her cheeks, if nothing else, as she answered, "It was fernseed. We aren't really supposed to have any, Corrie and I, because children aren't responsible enough to be able to become invisible at will, according to grownups. Father made the rule because Corrie got hold of some and went invisible when he was going to be punished for something. I only had a little bit left, and I haven't used it before for anything."

"I'm glad you *did* have it!" exclaimed Jasper. "Now, tell me the rest."

Rosemary did so, and there was a long silence afterwards, which she finally broke, to ask, "What are you thinking?"

"I'm thinking that the sooner I get you and the Eggchild to Father in Quarrine Castle, the better. If the Raiders are so desperate to have the Eggchild, *you* won't be safe now till we find out what it is, and why they want it."

"Why won't I?"

"Because you've shown them that you're able to protect the Eggchild from them. If you, a child, can do that, they certainly won't want our parents, with their power, to take care of it. You can't even go home now, and leave the Eggchild with me, because they must've worked out by now who's got it. If you reappear without it, you're their last link with it. How long do you think it'd be before they tried to kidnap you, to find out where you'd left the Eggchild?"

Rosemary's teeth chattered with sheer fright.

"I wouldn't have thought of all that! *What* am I going to do?"

3

Into the Forest

⊗

"Come to Quarrine with me, as I said," repeated Jasper. "At the moment, we've got the advantage. We know what you're like, but they don't know there are two of us now, do they? We know they've got magic power, and they probably guess that you have too, but they don't know about mine. We know not to trust them, after that senseless business in the stables. That was sheer devilry!"

Rosemary nodded, then realised Jasper couldn't see, so she agreed out loud.

"What now?" she asked quietly.

"Horses," muttered Jasper. "If we're going to make any speed to Quarrine, we've got to have horses, but where from?"

"Try the village green, Father used to have all the horses trained to make for the village if they threw a rider, or there was an accident, or something like that. Now their stable's burnt down, I expect that's where most of them will be."

"Good. Let's go. You carry the Eggchild. I can't manage it as well as the sack of food you brought me earlier on. It was bad enough getting this far."

"Jasper! You don't mean you wasted time finding the food while the stable was burning?"

"I don't know about 'wasted'! *One* can live off the land between here and Quarrine, but two can't. Does the Eggchild eat anything?"

"Doesn't seem to."

"That's a relief. We haven't got any milk, or anything like that. Come on, let's go and find those horses."

They moved quietly through a silent world. All the normal, small night-noises seemed to have ceased, and even the village was unnaturally quiet. They crept down the flower-bordered streets to the central green. It looked grey under the moon gleam, but here and there were large dark masses which moved and stamped nervously as they approached. Rosemary began to murmur soothingly as she angled towards her own little pony. Bramble raised her head to snuff the air as Rosemary came near, and even trotted forward, staring round anxiously, then twitched and sidled away as she felt Rosemary's invisible hand pat her neck.

Jasper was having more difficulty approaching Duke, the pony he'd chosen. The animal simply would not stay still. It had had one bad fright tonight already, and had no intention of standing and letting a thing which it couldn't see, but could smell, approach it.

Eventually, Rosemary gave the Eggchild to Jasper, mounted Bramble and managed to catch Duke.

While Rosemary was busy pony-catching, Jasper used the time to make a sling from his cloak so that either he or Rose could carry the Eggchild on their backs. It wasn't an easy job, tying invisible knots in invisible material with invisible fingers.

Rosemary came trotting back on Bramble, with Duke following.

"I've thought where we might be able to get two saddles," she said.

"Where?"

"Sam the groom lives down here. He often brings saddles home to mend in the evening. I know he's got one at the moment, and he might have two. They'll be in the shed at the bottom of his garden."

Jasper scrambled on to Duke's bare back, having handed the Eggchild to Rose. Duke didn't like having the sack of food banging his flanks, and shied half-heartedly as he followed Bramble across the green, and down a lane.

Rosemary tied Bramble to a fence on the right of the lane, and unlatched a wicket gate. She slipped into Sam's garden, and moments later a saddle and bridle came floating through the air towards Jasper.

"Put these on Duke. There's another in the shed." Rosemary was gasping for breath as she held the saddle up to Jasper.

"I'm not on Duke, chump! I'm just beside you. I'll do the lifting of the next one. You get on with saddling Bramble."

Rose did as she was told, but still only finished at the same time as Jasper. Bramble would blow out her sides so that she couldn't pull the girths tight, and she had to tickle her to make her snort the air out of her lungs. Usually it was a game they both enjoyed, but tonight, she wished the mare were less playful.

"I've got to leave a message for Mother," she announced suddenly. "If I don't, what's to stop her thinking the Night Raiders have got me, or that I was burnt in the fire?"

"Surely Lady Fenella won't even know about the Raiders? She didn't wake up and see them."

"No, she didn't! Neither did Corrie! D'you suppose they'll be gone by morning?"

"Sure to be, I think. After all, it's the Eggchild they seem to be interested in, not the Arbour."

"You mean, they'll be after us?"

"I'm afraid so, if they can find out which way we went." Jasper didn't add that their choice of direction would be easy to guess, since Quarrine Castle was the obvious place to go.

"I *have* got to leave a message then, or Mother'll never know what really happened."

"You're not going to wake Sam, are you?" demanded Jasper anxiously as the garden gate swung open again.

"Of course not, stupid. I'll leave a message with the flowers. It's just a case of finding a sensible kind."

"Oh. Well, I always think of roses as fairly levelheaded, and Sam's got plenty of those. Or lilies."

Rosemary evidently paused, because the gate stayed wide open.

"You're a very unusual person, Jasper."

"Me? Why?"

"You think about things. Not just your stones and metals, but other things too. You're quite right about roses, but I think the lilies would be better."

"Can I come and watch?"

"If you want to. But there'll be nothing to see."

There was a creaking of leather as Jasper dismounted, and he followed Rose into the garden.

Over by the housewall grew a tall clump of white arum lilies. The grass of the lawn in front of them flattened as Rosemary knelt down. In a slow, gentle voice, she repeated what had happened to her that night, and how she, Jasper and the Eggchild had escaped, and were heading for Quarrine Castle.

"Keep close watch for the Raiders, Mother. They are evil," she finished. The lilies swayed and rustled, and in the moonlight, Jasper saw a dark stain rise over the whiteness of the flowers.

"What colour are they now?" he whispered.

"Red. For a message of danger. Sam'll notice them, and know what it means. Mother'll have the message by noon tomorrow at the latest."

Together, they left the garden, and remounted the ponies. Rosemary settled the Eggchild on her back in Jasper's sling, and Jasper tied the sack securely to his saddle-bow. Clopping quietly, the two ponies followed the lane to its end in the open fields around the village, then went through the fields and into the Greathunt Forest. Jasper led the way, but he ignored the road to Quarrine, angling into the trees to the left of it.

"Where're we going?" called Rosemary softly.

"*My* way to Quarrine. If we're right about the Raiders wanting the Eggchild, they'll search the road, so we don't want to be seen on it when they do."

"Ugh! No!"

For over an hour, Jasper led through moon-dappled glades and under shadowy dark trees. Bramble seemed to be quite happy to follow Duke and his invisible rider, so Rosemary dozed as they jogged along. But the ache of her shoulders dragged her back to wakefulness and she hunched her back to ease the Eggchild's weight.

"Jasper?"

Duke ambled to a halt, and turned to face Bramble.

"What's the matter?"

"I can't go on much further tonight. It's going to rain within the next hour, and if we get wet, the fernseed'll wash off."

"So we'll be visible again?"

"Yes."

Jasper looked up. The horses had halted in a wide, grassy clearing. The sky was clear, bright, and star speckled. There wasn't a cloud to be seen. Rosemary could hear the frown in Jasper's voice when he demanded, "Why ever do you think it's going to rain?"

"I don't think. I know. I can't tell you how."

There was silence until Duke snorted, and stamped impatiently. He didn't like standing around in this open space.

"I don't think you can be right, Rose," said Jasper at last. "The place I want to get to is at least another hour's ride away, but I know we'll be safe to sleep when we get there, so I'd rather not stop now. I expect you'll find you're not as tired as you think you are, if we go on."

"Do you *want* us to become visible again?"

"Of course not. Not until we reach the Castle, in fact."

"Then why not stop now, instead of risking getting soaked?"

Too tired to be gentle any longer, Jasper snapped, "Oh, stop making getting wet your excuse, Rosemary! It's not going to rain within the next hour, or even the next *day* by the look of the sky. Give me the Eggchild to carry if it's bothering you, and let's move on!"

After this, nothing would have made Rosemary admit to tiredness, or give up the Eggchild, even if the sling on her back rubbed her into blisters. Her voice stiff as she held back hurt tears, she said, "I'm all right. Go on, then," and refused to speak again.

From the pace he set from then on, it was obvious that Jasper was annoyed. He did not pause for anything, but brushed past low-hanging branches, splashed across streams, and urged Duke into trotting up slopes as well as down into valleys.

Rosemary shivered, and pulled her cloak closer around her as a breeze began to rustle the leaves of the great trees. Before half an hour had passed, the breeze had strengthened to a gusty wind, which brought scudding clouds across the sky from the east. It seemed a good time for her to remember a lesson Lady Fenella had once spoken of to her daughter.

"Whether you are right or wrong, Rosemary, an angry or bitter word, once spoken, can never be taken back, but it will be remembered for a long time."

Rosemary contented herself with thinking of all the things she *could* have said if she hadn't remembered her mother's words. It would have been so easy to start making comments like, "Looks like rain, doesn't it, Jasper?" or, "What a lot of clouds and wind there are now. Who would have thought there could be rain, an hour ago?"

Rosemary felt a little bit ashamed of even thinking these things, though. Of course, Corrie would have believed her at once, but then, he already knew she was always right about when rain was coming. Jasper didn't know.

"But he'll believe me another time!" muttered Rosemary to herself. Her shoulders were rubbed sore by the sling by now, and Bramble was stumbling more and more often through sheer tiredness.

When the rain eventually started, Duke gave a sudden bound forwards, as though Jasper had just kicked his ribs, then settled back into the same jog-trot as before.

Both Rosemary and Jasper were dripping wet, and visible once more, by the time Jasper reined to a halt in a valley with a deep, slow-flowing stream at the bottom of it. They had been riding beside a cliff for some time, and Rosemary had been taking her mind off her own wetness by watching Jasper gradually reappear in front of her. At first, he was visible only in round coin-size blobs wherever a large rain-drop landed; then, as the downpour continued, the patches ran together and became the solid shape of Jasper, with black, slicked-down hair.

Abruptly, he wheeled Duke to the right, and disappeared again. It was only when Bramble reached the point where pony and boy had disappeared that Rosemary saw there was a huge, vertical split in the cliff. Jasper had ridden Duke through it, and dismounted in the dryness of a shallow cave.

Bramble stumbled into the deeper gloom too, and stood with hanging head and trembling legs.

Jasper brushed past without looking at Rosemary, ran down to the bank of the stream, and pulled a small stone out of the water. He came back with it, drawing his dagger as he did so. Rosemary's eyes ached as she tried to see what he was doing, but it was too dark. She heard a dragging, brushing sound, then several metallic snicks. Sparks darted before her eyes, then Jasper gave a grunt of satisfaction, and started blowing softly. A reddish glow lit the cave, spread, and caught as the boy piled on more twigs and, finally, branches, from a pile at the back of the cave.

In all this time, neither Rosemary nor Bramble

had moved, and Jasper left the fire to come over to them. He noticed what Rosemary herself was unaware of—she was swaying in the saddle through sheer tiredness. Her eyes looked black and bruised in a very white face.

"Give me the Eggchild, Rose," he commanded, holding up his arms.

"I can't," said Rosemary, in a perfectly clear, normal voice. "I can't move my shoulders," and she toppled sideways into Jasper's arms, fast asleep.

Calling himself all sorts of a fool, Jasper carried her over to the fire, and propped her up while he untied the sling. He was appalled when he saw the deep chafe-marks on her shoulders and back, but he had nothing to put on the blisters, so he just covered them with a clean handkerchief torn in half, and laid Rosemary as comfortably as he could by the fire, with the Eggchild beside her.

"Invisibility has its disadvantages," he told Duke, as he unsaddled him. "I snapped at her for giving me a warning which was true, and if I'd been able to see her, I'd have known half an hour ago that she was almost asleep in the saddle. At least she can sleep safely now, and I needn't disturb her until she wakes up naturally."

He rubbed the pony down with a handful of grass, then turned wearily to do the same for Bramble. As he rubbed the cream pony's flanks and legs, the Eggchild gave a sudden, tiny chirrup, and started to sing again. Jasper straightened with a sigh of relief.

"Now I *know* we're safe for a while," he muttered, and rolled up in his cloak to sleep. He was still wondering what to do in the morning about Rosemary's blisters when his thoughts whirled away into darkness.

4

The Shrimp

❧

Rosemary opened her eyes and rolled over, blinking blurrily. She yawned, then coughed until her eyes streamed, as she spat out the fire-wood ash she'd inhaled.

Wide awake now, she sat up. Hazily she remembered Jasper lighting the fire in whose ashes she seemed to be almost lying. Her clothes were dry, and the pain in her back and shoulders was completely gone. The Eggchild still lay beside her, crowing ·and singing happily. Its glow lit a small area of the cave, showing Jasper's rumpled cloak lying where he had slept, but there was no sign of the boy.

"Jasper?"

There was a scrambling noise from outside the cave, but Jasper didn't appear.

Too curious to be afraid, Rosemary jumped to her feet and ran forward across the sandy floor of the cave. She was just in time to see something small and pink plop into the water from the stream bank. Looking to either side, Rosemary could see Jasper a little way off, holding the bridles of the two ponies as they browsed.

"Jasper!" she called. Immediately, the boy looked round, raised a hand to wave, and came towards her. He tied the bridles to a rowan overhanging the stream, where the ponies could still snatch a few mouthfuls of grass, then came right up to her, and stood looking carefully at her.

"Before you say anything, Rose," he interposed, as she opened her mouth to speak, "I'm as sorry as I can be, about the way I spoke to you last night."

Rosemary grinned. Her resentment seemed very far away and long ago.

"That's all right, Jasper. I was very angry then, but I got over it."

Jasper looked surprised and a little envious. "You're much nicer than I am, Rose. When I'm angry, I say all sorts of things I don't mean."

"I *thought* a lot of nasty things," admitted Rosemary honestly, then repeated what her mother had told her. Jasper thought about the advice, but said he didn't know whether he'd remember it when he was in a temper, as she had.

"How're your blisters this morning?" he went on.

"What blisters?"

"Those huge blisters the sling rubbed on your shoulders and back."

"I haven't got any, Jasper. You're teasing me because I complained, aren't you?"

"No! Let me see your back."

Rosemary turned round, bent over, and pulled up her tunic, revealing a tanned, unmarked back. Jasper touched the knobs of the girl's backbone, and said in an odd tone, "Rose, last night there was a huge bleeding blister where each of your vertebrae sticks out, and there was a cut on each shoulder, where the sling dug in. I swear there was!''

Rosemary pulled down her tunic, and turned to see Jasper running his fingers through his thick black hair in a gesture of utter bewilderment.

"It must have been the Eggchild," she said matter-of-factly.

"That healed you?"

"Yes. After all, what do we know about it?"

"Nothing. Yes, I suppose you could be right."

"I'm not stiff after all that riding, either. Are you?"

"No. Talking of riding reminds me about the ponies. They woke me up this morning, stamping and tossing as though something had disturbed them. I couldn't see anything when I got up, though."

"That reminds me, too. I came out to look for you because I thought I saw something running away from the cave entrance when I woke up. It jumped in the stream."

"Where?"

Rosemary led the way to where whatever—it—was had plopped into the water. There was a shelf of rock there, overhanging a deep, still pool. In the sunlight, the pool bottom was speckled with light and shade. As the two faces appeared up above, a trout flicked under the overhang, and a large crayfish waved its antennae busily over the pebbles and moved to get out of sight too.

"Crayfish! There's our breakfast!" exclaimed Jasper, flinging off all but his trousers. He leapt into the water, spraying Rosemary with the flying droplets he raised, ducked under the surface, and grabbed the crayfish. It wriggled out of his grasp and beat a panic-stricken retreat towards a hollow in the bank.

"Jasper!" yelled Rosemary, pointing to the creature.

"What?" gasped Jasper, cross at having let it get away; then he saw what Rosemary had seen, and stood still.

The crayfish was undergoing the most amazing changes. It still scrabbled frantically to push itself into the hole, which was obviously much too small, but the head which butted at the bank was human one minute and crayfish the next. Then a claw would change to a hand, and back. The oddest combination came when the creature was crayfish to the waist, with human legs below.

While it was so preoccupied and bewildered, Jasper crept up behind it, and made no mistake when he grabbed it. He hauled it out of the water at a moment when the goggle-eyed head was human, and said, "Whichever you are, fish or human, make up your mind so we can talk to you!"

Once out of water, the mixed-up crayfish became an entirely human, very small boy, who opened his mouth, screwed up his eyes, and shrieked with terror.

"Don' cook me on the fire! *Please* don' cook me!"

"Poor little thing! You just come with Rosemary, and have some breakfast. Then you can tell us who you are, if you want to."

"Won't cook me?"

"Of course not! You're a little boy, and Jasper and I don't eat little boys."

"Oh." The child stuck a thumb in his mouth, around which had suddenly sprouted a set of whiskers like a seal's, and stared at Rosemary.

He reached out and touched her glossy curls consideringly and, immediately, the whiskers twisted into curls too. Jasper turned away to hide

his laughter, and Rosemary grinned as she asked,
"What's your name, boy?"

"Shrimp," said the boy, feeling the curls round
his mouth. He obviously felt there was something
wrong with them, because they disappeared again,
and he tucked a hand into Rosemary's.

"Breakfus?" he reminded her, and followed as
she led back to the cave.

He seemed rather nervous of Jasper as they
munched bread and jam from the supplies in the
sack, but his nervousness gradually wore off, par-
ticularly since he couldn't keep his eyes off the
Eggchild, and it was impossible to watch them
both at the same time.

After staring at it owlishly while he ate, the
Shrimp finally stood up, and walked over to the
Eggchild. He sat down beside it, and put his hands
on the glowing shell.

"*My* baby," he sighed with satisfaction, and
curled up with his arms around it.

Jasper and Rosemary stared at each other, their
expressions asking each other if this could be true.
Finally, Jasper whispered, "Find out what you
can. I'll go and saddle the horses ready to leave.
He'll talk to you, but he's still scared of me."

Rosemary nodded, and waited until Jasper had
gone out with the saddles and bridles before she
went over to the Shrimp.

"Why did you come out of the water to look at
me this morning, Shrimp?" she asked.

"Not you. It," replied the Shrimp, hugging the
Eggchild even harder.

"You mean you saw the Eggchild and came to
look?"

"This is *my* baby. Mamma said so," repeated
the Shrimp.

"Is that what she said?" asked Rosemary

gently. "Where is Mamma? Did you get lost?"

"No. Mamma went away. Nasty man came, and Mamma . . ." A crafty look came into the Shrimp's face. "Mamma turned him into a beetle." His face fell. "Then she went away. Ooh! Mamma! Want my Mamma!"

Suddenly the Shrimp was wailing his grief, and his shape-changes were completely uncontrolled. Rosemary wanted to cuddle and comfort him, but he changed so quickly into an eel, a crab, a seal, a dogfish, and a flounder that she really didn't see how she could. At last, though, the noisy sobs subsided, and the Shrimp fell asleep with one arm firmly round the Eggchild, and a thumb stuck in his mouth.

Rosemary stood up quietly, left the Shrimp with "his" baby, and went to find Jasper, who had finished saddling the horses long ago. He was idly turning over the stones in the bed of the stream, to see what the water had washed down from the hills. This reminded Rosemary of something she had meant to ask before.

"What did you dash out to the stream for, last night?"

"Flint. We haven't got a tinderbox between us, so I used flint and steel from my dagger to strike enough sparks to light a fire. Never mind that, though. What did you find out?"

"Not much," and Rosemary told him what the Shrimp had said.

"But he sticks to his point that it's *his* baby?"

"Oh yes. He's got no doubt about that."

"Hmm. This gets queerer and queerer. I mean, who'd abandon a—what do you reckon he is?— four-year-old child in a wilderness like this? And what did happen to his mother? Where is she? If we can find her, I suppose all our problems'll be over, because she could settle who or what the Eggchild is, straight away.''

"You don't suppose she could be Princess Diana of Argentia, or the wife of Old Sol? Nobody's ever seen her, only their son, Zonn.''

"Why ever should you think of them?''

"Isn't it obvious? Whoever the Shrimp's parents are, they must have as much Power as our parents. Can *we* change shape like the Shrimp?''

"No. True, but we can do other things.''

"Hmm. Jasper?''

"Yes?''

"You know a lot more than you're supposed to about what the Four Families can do, don't you?''

"I suppose I do. I never have been able to understand why we're not even supposed to admit to each other that we have unusual Powers. Why does it have to be such a secret?''

"I don't know. It's not a thing I think about very often—my own Power, I mean, and that's why I don't talk about it, not because I feel I shouldn't.''

"It's that way with me too. Knowing what the layers of stone beneath my feet are, as I walk over them, is as natural to me as eating or breathing. It was obvious last night that you felt the same way about knowing that there was rain coming. You *expected* to be believed, because you knew it was true. I *know* that about sixty feet straight down under where we're sitting is a thick layer of coal, but I'm not going to dig it up to prove I'm telling the truth.''

Rosemary smiled. "We'd be here for days, if you wanted to do that,'' she said.

"No we wouldn't. I'd shift the rock structure to make a hole down to it in about two hours.''

"Can you do that?''

"Easily."

Rosemary stared, remembering something.

"Then, when you said your father might cause an earthquake if he got angry, you *meant* it!"

"Course I did! It's been known to happen before."

Rosemary thought about having that kind of Power, and decided hers was an altogether gentler kind.

"What are we going to do about the Shrimp?" she asked.

"What can we do except take him with us to Quarrine? We can't leave him out here in the middle of the Forest."

"I think we ought to be going, don't you? How long till we get to the castle?"

"Another two days' travelling, I should think, because we can't travel fast. You go and wake the Shrimp, and I'll bring the horses. I've woven a basket for the Eggchild to lie in, and we can fix it to either Duke's or Bramble's saddle today. The Shrimp can ride with either of us."

Rosemary nodded absent-mindedly. "Who do you suppose the 'nasty man' was, that the Shrimp says his mother turned into a beetle before she went away?"

"Shall I tell you what I think? I think that young man made up the bit about changing into a beetle. I think it's what the Shrimp *wishes* had happened to his enemy. I've noticed my younger brother doing the same thing. He once told Father that he'd turned me into a pebble after I'd smacked him for something, but he hadn't really. He just wished he had."

"That's even worse!" muttered Rosemary, wandering off towards the cave. "That means the 'nasty man' may still be around somewhere. Ugh!

I wish we were safely in Quarrine Castle.''

"Don't we all!" agreed Jasper, glancing up at the cliffs on either side. There were a couple of things he'd noticed that morning that he had no intention of telling Rosemary. She was under enough strain already.

5

The Helpful Stranger

When he first saw the horses, and realised that he was supposed to ride one of them with Jasper or Rosemary, the Shrimp promptly turned into an eel, and wrapped himself tightly around Rosemary's ankle, while his two beady eyes assessed the ponies. It took patient coaxing on the girl's part to get him to unwind himself and even then he wouldn't settle to being completely human.

"Don't like them," he complained, pointing a flipper.

"Don't you want to come with us?" asked Rosemary.

"Where?"

"To see a big castle on a hill where there are kind people who can take care of you until you find your Mamma."

The Shrimp pondered, scratching behind an ear with a claw. Click, snick it went, then turned to a finger-snapping hand as he asked, "Any water?"

Rosemary shot an enquiring glance at Jasper, never having been to Quarrine Castle.

The older boy crouched to come down to the

Shrimp's level and said, "Lots of water, Shrimp.
The castle is on a hill, but the hill has its feet in the
water. The river flows right around the hill before
it goes on toward Argentia. There's a harbour
with lots of boats, big and little. Some have
coloured sails, or stripy ones. I'll take you out in a
rowing-boat, if you like."

"Promise?"

"Promise. Now, you ride with Rosemary on
Bramble." Jasper tried to pick the Shrimp up, but
the little boy kicked, and became tearful.

"No. Got my own. Put me *down!*"

Mystified, Rosemary asked Jasper, "Got his
own what?"

"How do I know?"

The Shrimp trotted over to the riverbank, by the
deep pool, and jumped in. Seconds later, he reappeared dragging behind him the large trout they
had seen earlier, but as soon as the fish's nose was
above water, it began to make the weirdest braying noises.

"It sounds like a donkey!" exclaimed Rosemary, and that, of course, was what the fish
turned out to be, once it was on dry land again.
The Shrimp came across to them, pulling the little
animal behind him.

"My donkey," announced the Shrimp, rather
unnecessarily, and scrambled into the saddle
which was already on its back.

"Ready," he grinned, then laughed at the other
two, who were still staring at him.

Rosemary blinked and turned away, still wondering whether she was imagining the docile little
grey animal she had seen pulled out of the water.
Jasper too was moving in a dazed sort of way
towards Duke. But they were getting so used to in-
credible things happening that by the time they
had ridden through the forest for a couple of

hours, they had accustomed themselves to hearing two pattering clops from the donkey for every stride taken by their own ponies.

"What's your donkey's name?" asked Rosemary.

"Trout," replied the Shrimp.

Jasper gave a whoop of laughter and spluttered, "Like master, like beast!"

The Shrimp didn't seem to be offended. "He's never sure which he is, really."

"I'm not surprised, if you often shape-change him to keep you company in the water."

"He's not a good trout."

"Why—"

"Acos even when he's a fish as soon as 'e puts his nose out of the water to catch a fly, he goes " 'EE-aw'."

"No wonder I thought I was going mad this morning. I kept on hearing something braying, over by the river. It must've been Trout."

"I speck so."

They ate lunch on a hill-top, having left the forest behind them. In front lay a country as crumpled as a piece of paper which has been crushed in the hand, and thrown down. To Rosemary's eyes, used as she was to the flat, gentle river-country of the Arbour, it looked a bleak wilderness of twisted valleys and hills, humping ever higher to the snow-capped mountains. But Jasper seemed sure of his way, even though there was not a track, village or house in sight, and he sat happily naming various landmarks until they had all finished eating.

The Shrimp and Trout, who followed his master like a dog, wandered off down the hill, among the scrubby bushes, while Rosemary packed up what they had not eaten.

"Jasper, the food sack's getting ominously

light, I'm trying to think what fruits are in season."

Silence fell while Rosemary thought, and they were both startled to hear a deep, gentle voice just behind them. "Can I be of any help to you, children? Have you wandered away from your parents, that you are so far from any habitation?"

Jasper and Rosemary whirled round, and saw a tall, brown-faced man astride a big chestnut horse. The horse's bridle was tooled with gold, and the man himself was richly dressed in a red tunic and hose, with matching leather knee-boots, and a voluminous purple riding-cloak. A feathered cap shaded his grey eyes, and his mouth was smiling. One hand rested lightly on the hilt of a long sword which was belted to his waist, and the hilt of a little silver dagger could be seen sticking out over the top of his left boot.

Feeling that they had had enough time to look at him, the stranger asked again, "Can I help you?"

When Jasper replied, Rosemary only just managed to prevent herself gasping with surprise, because he spoke with such a thick accent that she could barely understand him.

"Ah naw, thank 'ee, zur. I do 'ave brung this yong leddy aht fer the day. I baint lost. We'm goin' back to t' Deepdig mine over yonder s'arternoon. T'was kind in 'ee ter ax though."

"Oh. I see. I take it you're a miner then, lad?"

"Ah am that."

"Tell me, then, what do they mine at the Deepdig?"

"Feldspar, zur. T'stuff folks call blue-john on account o' t'colour of t'crystals."

For some reason, this answer seemed to annoy the stranger. He snapped, "Most interesting, young man.'' His eyes flicked from Jasper to Rosemary.

"I heard you mention fruit, my dear. If your mother asked you to pick some, you could gather the blackberries growing at the foot of this hill. I noticed a large patch of plump fruits there.''

"Thank you,'' smiled Rosemary gratefully, still inwardly puzzling over Jasper's odd behaviour.

"It's nothing,'' said the stranger, pulling on the reins of his horse.

"Please, zur. What may we call 'ee?''

The stranger stared at Jasper, and replied, "My name is Doppel.'' He nodded to the two children, twitched the reins of his tall mount, and cantered away down the hill in roughly the direction the children would be taking.

"Wasn't he handsome?'' said Rosemary, looking after him in admiration.

"Handsome is as handsome does,'' grunted Jasper obscurely, sprinting over to Duke and Bramble.

"What *is* the matter with you, Jasper? It was terribly rude of you to speak to Doppel the way you did.''

Jasper turned back to her, holding the Eggchild's basket in his arms. It had remained attached to Duke's saddle while they were eating lunch.

"Listen,'' ordered Jasper. Rosemary stared at him.

"I don't hear anything . . .'' she began, then her eyes fell on the Eggchild, and she understood.

"Oh.''

"Exactly. We *must* learn to notice, the minute it goes quiet.''

"You noticed?''

"Yes.''

"—And that's why you pretended you were an ordinary miner."

"Yes."

"D'you think he believed you?"

Jasper shook his head.

"I'd be very surprised if he did, but at least I didn't give him any excuse for staying with us."

Rosemary gulped down a lump which seemed to have jumped into her throat. Just as she'd got rid of it, and Jasper had re-strapped the Eggchild's basket to the saddle, the lump jumped back as something crashed out of the bushes, and cannoned into her.

A frantically butting head with long floppy ears turned out to belong to Trout. He grabbed Rosemary's jerkin in large yellow teeth, and pulled her desperately back towards the bushes. Fear clutching at her breath, Rosemary gasped, "Jasper, bring the horses and follow. I'll go with Trout. Hurry!"

She flung herself on to the little donkey's back, and drew up her knees to prevent her feet dragging on either side of him. Trout plunged into the scrub, and pelted downhill in a series of teeth-jarring bounds. At the foot of the hill, he picked his way into the middle of a large patch of luxuriant brambles, laden with luscious blackberries. In the midst of this tangle lay the Shrimp, flat on his back. His mouth and fingers were stained with blackberry juice, testifying to the number he had eaten. Now he appeared to be asleep, but when Rosemary knelt beside him to wake him up, he did not stir. His breathing was shallow, and his heart beat fast. When she rolled back his eyelids, his eyes were dark, with wide pupils. Kneeling there, frightened and worried, Rosemary sensed a wrongness about the thorny plants around her.

Quickly, her hands reached out, then slowly

spread in a series of gentle movements. Before Jasper's gaze, as he hastily brought the horses down the hill, the brambles faded, and took shape again as low, lushly-growing plants, each burdened with evil-looking, round, purple blackberries.

"Enchanter's Nightshade," murmured Rosemary.

"Sounds a remarkably suitable name!" muttered Jasper. "What can we do?"

Rosemary looked up at him.

"How much salt have we got?"

"About a handful. Why?"

"Bring the waterbottle, and put the salt in. Shake it up until the salt's all dissolved, then give it to me."

Jasper did as he was told, and handed the bottle to Rosemary, who had raised the Shrimp until he was propped against her knee.

Gently, she prised open the little boy's mouth, and held the waterbottle to his lips. Slowly, she tilted more and more of the salty water into his mouth, and waited. Then she quickly rolled the Shrimp to one side, and he was comprehensively and ingloriously sick.

With a sigh of relief, Rosemary wiped his face and mouth.

"Pick him up now, Jasper. He'll sleep for some time. Enchanter's Nightshade isn't as poisonous as Deadly Nightshade, but even so, he'd eaten a fair amount."

"Ee-ah, ee-ah, ee-ah—aaww!" brayed Trout mournfully, following Jasper as he carried the Shrimp away to a patch of grass on the hill-side. Without being told, Jasper knew Rosemary wanted to be alone for what she did next.

All that reached his ears was the low, sad-angry strains of the song the girl sang, but he did not

watch as the evil plants shrivelled and curled, and the ground around their roots cracked and powdered away. The earth itself became barren and arid, blighted by the worst punishment it was possible for Rosemary to inflict. Instead, Jasper prepared to leave once Rosemary came back, fastening the Eggchild's basket and the foodsack to Bramble's saddle so that he was free to carry the Shrimp with him on Duke. Trout stood by the Shrimp where he lay on the grass, and stared at his master, his long face looking even sadder than usual.

A startled "Eee-aw!" brought Jasper whirling round to look, and thankfully he noticed that the Shrimp had turned over on his side in a much more natural sleeping position.

"It's all right, Trout. The Shrimp's going to get better," he said aloud, and jumped again, as Rosemary's voice said, "Of course he is, but the sooner we get him to water, the better."

Jasper didn't speak again until they were on their way once more.

"Why get him to water, Rose?"

"Well, I made him sick, and that got rid of a lot of the poison, but he'd already begun to digest it. He needs to drink a lot now, and we've got no fresh water left. I thought that if we found a pool and laid him in it, he'd automatically change to a fish, and he'd be *breathing* water, which might be even better."

"That's well thought out. I know where there's a good pool, too. I was planning to camp there tonight anyway."

For the rest of the afternoon they urged the horses to as good a speed as could be managed, and left Trout to keep up as best he could. Whenever they came to a stream, they laid the Shrimp in it, and let him breathe water for about half an hour before going on again, and usually the little donkey caught up with them in these intervals.

In the early evening, they set the horses to climbing to the ridgetops for the night, out of the twisting valleys they had been following for the sake of the water they held. Duke and Bramble showed they enjoyed being back on springy turf by breaking spontaneously into a canter, which carried them all, by dusk, to a sheltered spot where a ring of pines protected a dewpond and an area of grass from all the winds.

Jasper fashioned himself a sling and went hunting, while Rosemary made the Eggchild comfortable under blankets and cloaks. She unsaddled Duke and Bramble, hobbled them, and turned them loose to graze, then did the same for a weary little Trout when he came tittupping through the gloom at last.

The Eggchild remained ominously silent, and Rosemary didn't let it out of her sight while she collected wood for a camp fire. Jasper came back with a skinned, spitted rabbit, and soon had it suspended above a licking fire of blue-burning fircones and resinous wood. Rosemary spiked the rabbit with marjoram and thyme which she had found in the grass, and hoped the herbs would add a pleasant flavour to the meat.

The Shrimp chose his moment to wake up very well. Jasper had lifted him out of the dewpond only a few minutes before, and the rabbit was done to a turn. The little boy stirred, blinked and sat up, saying drowsily, "Mamma? Nasty man came again . . . Mamma?"

Rosemary glanced at Jasper to see whether he had heard what she had. He nodded without saying a word.

"Not Mamma, just Rosemary, Shrimp."

The tone was reassuring, but the Shrimp opened

his mouth, ready to give a wail. With great presence of mind, Jasper popped a juicy morsel on to the little boy's tongue, and the wail never sounded. His mouth shut like a trap, and he swallowed.

"Good," he muttered, feeling his tummy. "My belly's as flat as a flounder!" and he held out his hands for more meat.

"You *are* rather empty," agreed Jasper, grinning secretly at Rose, and he handed the Shrimp a leg of the rabbit to chew. They were all so hungry that table manners were abandoned that night. The rabbit was literally torn to pieces, and the gnawed bones thrown on the fire.

The Shrimp stayed awake only long enough to fill his stomach, then rolled up next to the Eggchild. His cheeks were still flushed, but within half an hour the Eggchild seemed to be working its healing magic, and he slept peacefully and healthily.

6

Dawn Encounter

Jasper and Rosemary slept as soundly as the Shrimp for a while, but again the plants woke the girl to warn her of danger. Her reflex action was to freeze like a frightened animal, all except for one foot, which lashed out at Jasper. The kick was not gentle, and Jasper woke with a yell.

"What . . . ?" he began, and rolled over.

"Where is the Egg that sings?" hissed Doppel softly, the tip of his sword twitching to and fro beneath the children's noses.

Rosemary realised that the Eggchild must be completely hidden under the Shrimp's blanket, but she knew that Doppel would soon discover it.

"Where is it?" he repeated.

The children could see his pale eyes gleaming in the moonlight, flickering from Jasper to Rosemary and back again. This was not the charming stranger of the day before, but a man possessed and twisted by a demonic emotion. Jasper, less paralysed by fear than Rosemary, had been watching Doppel carefully, and suddenly he raised a heel, and thumped it back to the ground. A shock wave rippled through the earth, and Doppel staggered.

"Grab the Eggchild and run for the trees," hissed Jasper, and was relieved to see Rosemary move as quickly as thought. Jasper himself picked the Shrimp up bodily, and flung him into the nearby dewpond, where he immediately disappeared underwater. But he didn't have time to get away himself. A cold, strong hand grabbed his shoulder in a cruel grip, and swung him round to face the sword and Doppel's eyes again.

"So! We have yet another brat with Powers I did not expect to find in one so young. Which brood do you belong to, I wonder? Quarrine? Yes. It must be Quarrine after that rigmarole you told me this morning. How *dare* you pit your puny Powers against mine? One day I will rule you all . . . One day *soon*." For a moment Doppel's gaze grew opaque, as though he were picturing those days to come. Then his grip on Jasper's shoulder tightened and his eyes seemed to bore into the boy's head.

"Where has she taken the Egg that sings? Beware, boy. I am not to be trifled with. I too have Powers."

"Find her yourself," retorted Jasper stonily.

The flat of Doppel's sword caught him a ringing blow across the side of his head, and Jasper would have fallen, except for that punishing grip on his shoulder. He tried to stamp again, but he seemed unable to move a muscle. Only his head could move.

"I'll never tell you!" he shouted, then kept silent, biting his tongue, as Doppel moved about him, delicately slashing his clothes so that the tip of his sword flicked to within a hairsbreadth of his shrinking body time and time again, yet never actually touching or breaking the skin. The·sweat of fear soaked Jasper, and there was nothing he could do to help himself. All the time, Doppel was hissing, "Where is it? Tell me and I'll stop. I'll give you riches beyond your dreams, power beyond your dreams, power beyond imagining. Only tell me where to find the Egg that sings. I will find it, whether you tell me or not, but you can save me time. Where *is* it?" Doppel's voice rose to a shriek of frustration as Jasper remained silent.

The boy was watching a thick rope of bindweed creeping over the grass from the direction of the trees. The creeper was thick enough to tie a man securely, or just trip him up.

"What can I do?" thought Jasper despairingly. "Even if Rose's trick does work, and the creeper tangles him up, I'm still stuck like this."

Then, from the deep blackness under the trees, a lighter shadow detached itself. It was behind Doppel, and Jasper watched it warily. Maybe this was some new devilry.

A few feet behind Doppel, the shadow halted, and a deep resonant voice said bitterly, "Pick someone your own size for a quarrel, Doppel. I've been following you all day."

With a cry of mingled fury and apprehension, Doppel whirled round, sword held at the ready.

"You cannot kill me," he mocked, "and you won't save the boy. *Nothing* can stop me gaining the Egg that sings."

Wearily, the voice replied, "It's always the same excuse! There is no Egg that sings. It does not exist." And with a cry, the newcomer leapt forward. Sparks flew in the darkness as the long swords rang together. As soon as Doppel's attention was diverted from him, Jasper found he could move, and he sprinted for the cover of the trees, his tattered clothes fluttering. In the darkness it was hard to tell how the fight was going, but if the cries and yells of fury were anything to go by, battle was fast and bitter.

Gradually, the noise moved away, as though one assailant was driving the other ever backwards, and Jasper risked calling to Rosemary. She answered from away to his left. Jasper had only just rejoined her when the most eerie, ululating scream rent a momentary silence, bringing tears of pity and fear to Rosemary's eyes.

The sky was paling to dawn by now, and the two clung together, neither willing to venture out into the clearing again. They waited, listening so hard they felt sure their ears must be pricked and pointed like a wary animal's.

A rustling sounded in the undergrowth away on the far side of the clearing, and a dark shape emerged on all fours from the deep blackness under the trees. The light was sufficient now to show a dark, animal-like bulk which shuffled painfully forward towards the pool of water, which glinted like a sheet of silk, reflecting the increasing light in the sky. The creature gasped and snorted at every step.

"Is it a bear?" whispered Rosemary fearfully.

"No. A man. But which one?"

A deep groan was torn from the figure out on the grass.

"Oh, water, come to me . . . I can't come to you. . . ." The voice was deep and soft, but the words were followed by a quick, "Ach!" as if something had suddenly hurt him.

"It's no good. Are you me, or am I you? Which one is real? I have killed you again, Doppel, but you've . . . you've done the same for me."

The tears were streaming down Rosemary's face. The voice was so regretful in its mourning.

"Oh . . . children . . . my own little ones, where are you? What did he do . . if only I knew! My wings . . . if only I had them, but they went long ago, when *he* first appeared.'' There was a short silence, then, ''Soft grass, a new dawn. What more could a man want? *I want my memory and the name the Enchanter stole from me*! He can't be dead. If he were, I'd know who I am. Oh . . . don't let me die not knowing who I am . . . !'' The voice died away again, and then Rosemary was running over the grass with the Eggchild in her arms. With a cry of alarm, Jasper bounded after her, and stood by her as she lifted the stranger's head into her lap. But there was no treachery here. The man was unconscious.

''Keep the Eggchild by him,'' ordered Rosemary, her nimble fingers laying bare an ugly wound low down beneath the man's heart. She showed Jasper where to press to slow the pumping bright blood, and he took her place, while she rushed off to search for what she needed among the grasses.

> *Cobwebs, woundwort and self-heal;*
> *In upland grass, for wounds from steel*
> *Search for blue spikes of self-heal.*

Even as she said the remember-rhyme, she was plucking the purply-blue heads of the flowers.

''The country lanes will heal a hurt, with crimson-purple furred woundwort. Mmm. No good up here, then. We're too high. Ah, cobwebs!''

She snatched a handful from branches and bushes, and trotted back to the clearing. Gently, she stretched layer after layer of gossamer across the ragged hole in the man's chest, and the blood-flow halted. As quickly as possible, Rosemary made a poultice from the self-heal, and slapped it, sticky-wet, over the cobwebs.

"What now?" queried Jasper.

"Get him to Quarrine Castle as quickly as we can, of course," snapped Rosemary. Blood didn't upset her, but too much had happened now in too short a time. The strain was beginning to tell on her. "Get the Shrimp out, will you, Jasper, and saddle the horses."

"Right," agreed Jasper, and left her with her patient.

The face Rosemary gazed anxiously at was not prepossessing. Dark eyebrows slanted across his forehead, meeting in a deep frowning "v" between his closed lids. The lashes were long and dark too, lying shadowy on hollow, deathly-white cheeks. From between the eyes jutted what could only be called a beak of a nose, curving out and down, giving the face something of the look of a bird of prey. The mouth was thin-lipped and cruel, but now drawn down pathetically at the corners in utter weakness.

Rosemary was glad when Jasper came back with Trout, Bramble and Duke ready saddled. The Shrimp held back, still sleepy and afraid to come near the strange man lying so still.

The Eggchild was strapped in its basket on Duke, and Jasper and Rosemary between them managed to heave the man into the saddle. It was an exhausting task, and they had to use the rope of bindweed to tie him on. They were reassured when the Eggchild began to sing again, but very, very softly, as though it were using most of its energy for something different.

Jasper and Rosemary doubled up on Bramble, the Shrimp mounted Trout, and they left without further talk. The older children were too worried, and the Shrimp too frightened, to speak to each other, and they rode all day without stopping for more than ten minutes at a time.

By mid-afternoon they were following a high-way beside the Opal River, but the emptiness of the road only increased Jasper's anxiety. Normally, there would be packtrains travelling to or from the mines night or day on this road. But not today.

When they came to the town, the harbour on the river was deserted, all but the small coracles for river fishing having gone elsewhere. The houses were shut up and quiet, and when they finally came to a wary halt after climbing the long slope to the castle gates, the portcullis was down, and the massive iron gates behind were shut.

"Who denies entrance to Jasper Sard?" yelled Jasper at the top of his voice.

An arrow tip was poked through a slit in one of the gate towers, and a face showed palely in the gloom behind the bow.

"Who goes there?" came a wary growl.

"Jasper Sard and friends."

"Identify your party by name."

"Lady Rosemary Moschatel of the Arbour rides with me. On the donkey is a child known as the Shrimp. On the other horse is a gravely injured stranger."

"Password?"

"How should I know the week's password? I've been away for three weeks!"

"I have orders to admit no one who doesn't know the password."

Jasper lost his temper. "Very well, then, soldier. You pay the price of denying me my own home!"

He dismounted, and began stamping hard on the ground. The earth where the horses and Trout stood was still, but the gatehouse and the port-cullis shivered and trembled as the shock waves travelled through the ground.

"Enough!" came a yell from within the gate-house.

Jasper paused. The portcullis lifted, and one of the huge gates swung open. Just inside stood a tall squarely built man with a rough-hewn face, whom Rosemary recognised immediately as Lord John Sard. He was frowning at Jasper, so to prevent any argument at the start, Rosemary tumbled off Duke into his arms, with a cry of "Uncle John! Oh, please get the doctor to look at this man. He's badly hurt, and I could only do very rough first-aid on him. He may even be dead."

Lord John was a sensible man. He sent one guard running for helpers with a stretcher, dispatched another to fetch the doctor, and himself untied the still unconscious stranger on Duke's back. He started back for a moment when he found the Eggchild in its basket, then lifted the stranger gently on to the stretcher. The doctor and his patient disappeared into one of the towers, and Lord John led his son and his guests through the main hall and up into the family living-room.

Lady Amethyst was there, calmly sewing, but she jumped to her feet at the sight of her tattered and weary son.

"What happened to your clothes, Jasper?" she asked.

"That's part of a very long story, Mother. Could someone bring up some food while we tell you what happened? Rose and I can stay awake, but I don't think the Shrimp can." He pointed to the little boy, who was clinging to Rosemary's hand. Lady Amethyst produced a wicker basket with a blanket in it from somewhere, and the Shrimp lay down and slept, curled up in front of the log fire.

Jasper set down the Eggchild's basket beside him and, when the food arrived, he and Rosemary told the story of their adventure from beginning to end.

"What do we do now?" asked Jasper.

"Sleep, my son," advised Lord John. His blue eyes twinkled. "Your tale needs much thought, and you and Rosemary need rest. I will think, while you two sleep. Maybe your mother and I will go and see this mysterious deliverer of yours, too. There are several things about him that I do not understand."

7

Treachery

Rosemary did not get an unbroken night's sleep. Towards dawn, she woke up as something long and slippery coiled itself round her ankle under the bedclothes. But this time, she wasn't frightened.

Quickly lighting her candle, she sat up, flung off the sheet which covered her, and stared at her feet, meeting the beady gaze of the clammy eel round her ankle.

"What's the matter, Shrimp?" she whispered. "Were you lonely?"

It took the Shrimp a few seconds to make himself human again, and even then, he couldn't quite hold his shape.

"Somebody in my room!" he whimpered, sucking his thumb vigorously, and blinking his sandy eyelashes at the light.

"Who?" gasped Rosemary, quickly sliding out of her bed, and bolting the door.

"Don't know!" wailed the Shrimp, flinging himself into her arms.

She soothed him, and gradually pieced the story

together. The chilling thing, to her, was that it so closely matched the search of her own home which had started this bewildering adventure.

Someone had crept into the Shrimp's room and put a hand over his mouth. The Shrimp promptly turned into a shark, and bit his unknown attacker. The man yelped, swore and let go, and the Shrimp dashed down the corridor to Rosemary's room, and dived under the bedclothes.

"You're sure it was a man?"

"Yes. Smelled of horses and sweat."

That seemed clear enough. Rosemary sat and cuddled the Shrimp, thinking of the long passageways between their guest-rooms and the Sard family's rooms, and knowing that she didn't have the courage to unbolt the door and go for help. There might still be someone prowling around.

Both children froze as the door handle clicked and moved up and down. The bolt held firm against a gentle thrust.

"Who's there?" called Rosemary shakily.

The door handle stopped moving, but there was no reply. The children stayed huddled together until morning, when a maid came with hot water for washing, and clean clothes for them to wear.

While they were all eating breakfast Rosemary told Lord John what had happened, and the first thing he did was to check that at no time had the guard outside the sickroom door been asleep or away during the night. The guard answered that he had been on watch all the time, but he had thought, round about dawn, that there was someone lurking in the darkness down the corridor.

At this, Lord John looked angry and worried too.

"It seems the enemy is within the gates already, as well as outside," he murmured. "Why, though? What do they want?"

"You know what Doppel said, Father, about

ruling us all . . ." began Jasper, but got no further. A bent old woman came in with a tray of hot drinks, and the Shrimp gave her one frightened glance, and shrieked with terror. Again and again he screamed, even while he hysterically changed into a bewildering succession of shapes.

Rosemary ran to comfort the little boy, but the Shrimp was too upset even to recognise a friend, and he eel-wriggled under the sofa, and stayed there, whimpering.

"Get out, Nutmeg," ordered Lord John to the serving woman, and she turned to go, meeting Rosemary's eyes as she did so.

The agony of hurt in the old woman's gaze brought tears to Rosemary's eyes, but then she looked again at the Shrimp curled up in a tight ball under the sofa, and ran over to kneel beside him.

Lord John's face was thunderous. "If *only* that child were older, he could give us the answer to all our questions. What in the world d'you suppose caused that outburst?"

"It couldn't have been Nutmeg who went into the Shrimp's room?" suggested Jasper.

"Smelling of horses and sweat? Anyway, Rosemary says the attacker swore when the Shrimp bit him, so the child must have heard his voice. He knows it was a man."

They all nodded, carefully not looking towards the sofa, where Rosemary was gradually coaxing the Shrimp out.

"What do we do now?" asked Jasper to fill the awkward silence, and his mother answered.

"You stay in the castle until your stranger has recovered enough to answer some of our questions, at least. We have already been threatened by the Night Raiders—that's why all the townsfolk are inside the castle. When they find out—if they find out—that we now have their precious Egg that sings, they'll try to carry those threats out.

The man you met—Doppel—must be their leader,
and he evidently dreams of power, and power
alone. Some way must be found to defeat him utterly, to save the country of the Four Families. If
only there were some way of letting Princess Diana and Old Sol know of the danger, so that
they could raise the people of Argentia and
Sunholm to defence.''

"You mean, between them, they could affect
the Raiders through moon-weather at night, and
sun-weather by day?" asked Jasper doubtfully.

"Jasper!" snapped Lord John, in sharp rebuke.
"We do *not* talk about our . . . our . . .''

"Power," supplied Rosemary, helpfully, but
only got a frown for reward.

". . . our *talents*," corrected Lord John heavily.
"Careless talk leads to misunderstanding and
jealousy—"

"Whereas silence only leads to more ignorance
and silly mystique!" growled Jasper.

Father and son glared at each other until Lady
Amethyst interposed. "Are you going, either of
you, to suggest a way to contact Princess Diana
and Old Sol?"

"I could go," offered Jasper. "I know my way
to the Silver Palace, and to Sunholm."

Lord John and Lady Amethyst looked at their
wanderer son with a queer mixture of disapproval
and grudging respect.

"No doubt you do, my son," commented Lord
John, "but you remain in this castle. Trial though
you are to me, if you should be taken and held
hostage I should be hard put to it not to agree to
terms to get you back."

The tone had been light, but the meaning was
not, and Jasper had the grace to look uncomfortable.

"No," continued Lord John. "What I must do

is think hard how to contact the other two Families, warn Princess Diana of possible threat to Selena and Old Sol of danger to Zonn, and suggest that we all gather at Mootmeet for a Council, as soon as possible.''

"What about Madam-mother?" asked Rosemary.

Lord John looked at his wife, and smiled.

"You must know, Rose, that your Aunt Amethyst came from the Arbour to be my wife, long years ago. She retains some of her talents, and she has a special link with your mother. Amethyst and Fenella have always been as close as sisters could be, who now live so far apart."

"Does Aunt Amethyst send messages to that strange flower in Mother's room that never dies?" asked Rose in wonderment.

There was no reply, but Lady Amethyst smiled as the three children went out, Jasper and Rosemary taking it in turns to carry the Shrimp piggyback.

Lady Amethyst's herb garden seemed to be the only empty place in the overcrowded castle, and the Shrimp quickly calmed down among the pleasant smells and peace of the enclosure. The children sat for a while on the camomile lawn, with their backs against the sun-warmed stones of the tower which backed the garden. Jasper talked quietly to the Shrimp, looking every so often at Rosemary, who sat gazing up at a clump of crimson wallflowers which grew out from the wall, just below some shuttered windows. He did not want to break her concentration, but when she frowned and glanced aside at him, he raised his eyebrows enquiringly.

"Keep an eye on the Shrimp, will you, Jasper? Don't let him out of your sight for a moment." She looked up again. "The scent of wallflowers is the scent of summer, to me. I love them, and so they make the effort to tell me things, even though they're not very clever. I must go and see the stranger. The flowers tell of fear and anguish inside the shuttered room.'' Abruptly her voice dropped. ''I'd go even if I wasn't worried about the stranger. The flowers say that one watches us wherever we go in the castle.''

''Don't be daft!'' muttered Jasper back. ''I expect Father's told a guard to keep an eye on us.''

''Jasper! You'll have to accept that good plants are incorruptible. They know evil. They wouldn't warn me against a guard of your father's.''

Jasper shrugged. ''You know best, I suppose. I don't like to think of treachery in the castle.''

''I don't think we're in danger at the moment. . . . Anyway, I must go and see what the trouble is in the sickroom. Take care.''

Rosemary got to her feet, ran over to the Shrimp, who was rolling like a cat in Lady Amethyst's carefully tended bed of mint, and said in a normal tone, ''I've got to go into the castle for a while, Shrimp dear. Stay and play with Jasper, like a good boy. I'll be back soon.''

''All right, Rosie,'' agreed the Shrimp, still rolling busily to release the cool, sharp scent of mint into the air.

Rosemary quietly went out through the wicket gate in the garden wall, casting a quick glance to either side as she did so. There was no one to be seen, but she realised unhappily that there were a number of windows which overlooked the herb garden. Any one of them could hide behind it the face of an enemy.

Wasting no time, Rosemary made her way up the winding staircase to the tower-room which housed the injured stranger. A guard leapt to his feet as she approached down the short corridor, and said sternly, "What're you doing here, maid? Lost your way?"

"I'm not a Quarrine girl, guard," replied Rosemary. "I'm Rosemary Moschatel of the Arbour, and I'd like to see the stranger."

"Your pardon, little lady, but how do I know you're telling the truth?"

Rosemary dimpled and said, "What's your favourite flower, soldier?"

"Well—I grow a lot of jessamine in my back garden . . ."

As he spoke, Rosemary's hands moved through the air, and she said, "Let me make you a present from your back garden, soldier."

The sweet scent of jasmine filled the air, and Rosemary pointed at the guard's pike where it leaned against the wall. Wondering, the soldier picked it up and sniffed at the white starry flowers which twined round the butt as far as the spearhead.

"I believe you, ma'am," he said, opening the door, "and . . . . thanks for the gift. I miss my garden."

Rosemary smiled again, and went into the sickroom. The stranger was lying flat on a low bed, his head turned towards the dim light of a lantern. The smell of sickness was in the air. He looked up as Rosemary came in, and smiled, as if to say, "You look nice, and I think I ought to know you, but I don't."

The first thing Rosemary said was not "How are you?" but "Don't be afraid. I'll open the shutters. You're not in a cage." She walked to the windows and flung back the wooden shutters, letting in a flood of sunlight, and mingled wallflower and mint scent from below. The sick man took a deep breath, shuddered, and said, "Thank you, little maiden. I smell wallflowers."

Rose nodded. "They're growing on the wall outside. I like their scent. It's warm and dusty and summery."

"I love them too. I wonder . . ." His eyes clouded, and he left the sentence unfinished.

Rosemary looked at him, suddenly filled with love for this stricken man. She seemed to understand what he was thinking and feeling, as if she'd known him for years.

"You wonder where you learned to love flowers."

The man nodded, unsurprised. Quietly, he said, "You tended me yesterday, didn't you?"

"Yes. I thought you'd die. Now, I don't think you will."

"No," he agreed, lightly touching the bandages over his wound.

"Whom were you fighting?" asked the girl, wondering whether he could tell any more than the little they already knew about Doppel.

"Myself," he replied savagely.

Rosemary didn't know what to make of this answer, so she said practically, "That's not possible. You didn't give yourself that wound."

"No," he agreed. "I didn't. I've fought the same man before. I'm a better swordsman than he is, and I kill him every time we meet, but soon I see him again, alive and well, and we fight again." He swept a hand across his face as if to wipe away a bad dream. "It's *not* an enchantment, or a delusion. I know I kill him, child. The first time this happened, I wasn't sure, so the next time I stabbed him to the heart to be certain, and for a wonderful moment, I remembered all those things I know I forget while he's alive. I knew who I am, and what I must do, where I came from, and where I was going. I was *whole*—just for a moment. Then, even as I cleaned my sword and sheathed it, ready to begin, I forgot again, and went on wondering. It's a nightmare, child; a nightmare which recurs every time I fight and kill him.''

"My name's Rosemary, and I'm ten," said Rose, thinking it would be best if he stopped talking now. He might fret himself into a fever.

"I'm glad to know you, Rosemary. I wish I could tell you my name, too.''

"I call you Hawk, to myself,'' said Rose, sitting down on the bed beside him.

"Hawk,'' he muttered, and again, "Hawk. I think—I think my name is something like that, but not quite. There are so many things I've forgotten. Sometimes, I dream about children, and wonder whether they are *my* children, and I see such a beautiful woman, too, with silver fair plaits which hang long down her back. Her eyes are dark blue and lovely, and her walk is a glide.''

Rosemary was enthralled, but she asked practically, "What did the doctor put on your wound?''

Hawk pulled a face and said, "Some evil-smelling sticky mess which I didn't like the look of,'' then he joined weakly in Rosemary's peal of laughter.

"Patients *never* like what's best for them," she said, and got up to go.

Hawk laid a hand on her arm. It looked very brown against her light golden tan.

"Rosemary, you brought the sunshine to this room, and I'm grateful, but may I tell you what *would* do this patient good?''

Her face gentle, Rosemary nodded.

"Bring me the Sun-babe who sang me back to life yesterday. I never believed Doppel when he ranted about the Egg that sings. Every time I fight him, he says something about wanting it, but I'd never seen it, and I took no notice . . . Whatever he wants it for, the reason can't be good. It *must* be kept away from him!''

In his agitation, Hawk was trying to sit up, so Rosemary assured him that she would ask whether the Eggchild could be brought to his room, and left him resting more quietly.

Within ten minutes she was back, with Lady Amethyst and the Eggchild. Hawk held out eager arms for the Eggchild, and struggled to sit up. Rosemary and Lady Amethyst lifted him gently, and propped him against pillows, then watched. The Eggchild glowed like a small sun, and crowed with happiness, convincing Lady Amethyst immediately that there was nothing to be feared from this man.

Hawk looked up, and said wonderingly, ''Now I have seen it, I feel I should know what this child is. Maybe I *have* seen it before: I've forgotten so many other things. What is it? *Why* can't I remember?''

Lady Amethyst slowly shook her head, unable to answer any of his questions.

Hawk bent his cruel-looking face over the Eggchild again. ''It heals me, and I feel—safe—for the first time in so long.''

They left him alone, with the Eggchild pressed to the bandages round his chest, and Rosemary took the opportunity to ask Lady Amethyst about the old servant woman. It seemed there was little to tell. Nutmeg had been working in Quarrine Castle for nearly a year. She never talked about herself or where she came from, but since she had proved to be utterly reliable and trustworthy, nobody ever asked her personal questions. Rosemary went back to Jasper and the Shrimp, still baffled by the look of pain in Nutmeg's eyes during the unpleasant scene at breakfast, and worried by the wallflowers' warning.

All that day, Jasper and Rosemary kept the Shrimp happy, but never let him out of sight; Hawk grew stronger by the hour as the Eggchild did its healing work; and an uneasy calm lay over the castle. By evening, even Jasper was prepared to admit that he could feel an uncomfortable prickle between his shoulder-blades wherever he went, as though someone were watching him. Lord John told him he was imagining things, and sent all three children off to bed.

Rosemary and the Shrimp had been moved into a room next to Jasper's, and the older boy woke Rosemary just as the sky was beginning to get light.

He held a hand to her mouth, and whispered, "We were right. There *are* enemies in the castle. The guard outside the sickroom's been found tied up and gagged. He's telling Father what happened, now. Come quickly, and listen. We're supposed to be asleep still."

"Hawk?" whispered Rosemary as she followed him.

"Gone. And the Eggchild."

8

The Swanship

❧

"I don't know what hit me, sir," muttered the guard, ruefully. His wrists and ankles were swollen where ropes had bitten in, and he had a lump on his head the size of a pigeon's egg.

"Never mind *what* hit you! *Who* hit you?" demanded Lord John. He had hastily thrown a robe over his nightshirt, and his wiry hair was still sleep-rumpled.

"Well, you see, sir, these two guards came up to me, dressed in our uniform. I didn't recognise either of 'em but we've taken on men from the town since all the folk came inside the castle. . . . Anyway, I challenged 'em, and they gave me the right password, so I said, 'What's up, mates?' and one of 'em replied, 'Order came from Lord John to move the stranger to a more comfortable room.' 'Seems an odd time to move 'im,' I said, but then t'other chipped in, 'Lord John doesn't want him seen by too many folk, see?' So I turned away to open the door, and that's when they hit me. I had my mail hood on, so I didn't completely keel over, but when everything stopped spinning I was as neatly tied up as a birthday present.''

Lord John nodded, though the silent children just outside the half-open door couldn't see this.

"Did they say anything else, do you remember?" he asked.

"Well, that's another funny thing, sir. What with the thundering in my head, I can't be too sure, but I've a feeling that when they ran into the sickroom, one of 'em yelled, 'He's away already with the child. He still has power to call on the son of the wind, curse them both!' I could be wrong about that, sir.''

"Whoever, or whatever, is the son of the wind?" pondered Lord John. "And how did he, or it, enable Hawk and the Eggchild to escape their enemies?''

There was silence, then Lord John got up, his chair making a loud scraping noise in the quiet, and said, "You have nothing to be ashamed of, soldier. You did what you could . . . Yes? You have thought of something else?''

"Yes, sir. I've got a definite idea there're more of 'em among your guards. One of 'em said, 'We must report back to Doppel,' and the other replied, 'Well, there're others to take care of the child, and keep watch here.' I kept my eyes shut when they came back into the passage. I pretended I was out cold.''

The soldier sounded half-ashamed, so the children were glad to hear Lord John repeat his reassurance. Then he ordered a search-party to comb the castle for Hawk, the Eggchild and the two attackers, and a second party to make ready to search the countryside surrounding the castle.

Jasper tugged Rosemary's arm, and pointed back to the bedrooms. They crept into Rosemary's room, and closed the door softly.

"We've got to get the Shrimp to safety, and

find Hawk and the Eggchild,'' said Jasper urgently. "You heard what the soldier said. If there're other disguised Night Raiders in the castle, they can kill the Shrimp almost any time they choose. We'll be safer outside these walls than in!''

"The Eggchild. What about the Eggchild?'' whispered Rosemary. "Where could Hawk have taken it, and—how did he get away?''

"You're like me—taking it for granted Hawk's not hiding in the castle somewhere?''

"No. He's not in the castle. I feel sure of that. I don't know why, but suddenly I feel trapped here. I want to be out, away from these walls.''

"What can the son-of-the-wind be?'' wondered Jasper, then snapped his fingers.

"Rose, if we're really leaving the castle, we've got to go *now*. I know a way. While I pack some food and bedrolls, you get dressed, and get the Shrimp up. Then, while I dress, you leave the Shrimp with me, and see whether you can reach the sickroom without being seen. Maybe the wallflowers can tell you how Hawk and the Eggchild left that room.''

Rosemary did as she was told, and by the time she was back Jasper and the Shrimp were ready. Breathlessly, she whispered, "All they could tell me was that whatever-it-was had huge wings, and Hawk and the Eggchild flew away on its back.''

"That's what we needed to know. They'll be miles away by now, but we must find them before Father's search-party does. He can't be sure there're no Raiders amongst the guards he chooses for the search, and goodness knows what could happen to Hawk and the Eggchild if they . . . No. *We* must find them, and take them on to Mootmeet and hope they'll be safe there.''

The Shrimp had fallen asleep again, so Jasper

picked him up, folded in a blanket. Rosemary swung the pack of food and the bedrolls on to her back and followed him to the door, only to bump into him as he halted abruptly.

Outside the door stood old Nutmeg. Her wrinkled face was brown and withered, but her eyes twinkled bright blue as she smiled.

"Take care, and go in safety, children. You're right to trust your instincts. You are not safe within these walls. I could tell you . . . oh, much, if only I could remember *half* of what I've forgotten."

"Let us past, Nutmeg," said Jasper roughly, tired of the old woman's mumblings. As he strode past her, Nutmeg laid a hand on his arm, and said suddenly and clearly, "Hawk is in the Place of Dragons. Look for him there, but beware of him. When the Enchanter is near, Hawk cannot hear reason until he has fought him. Save him if you can, children. Prevent the fight, for the next one will be the last, for good or evil."

"How do *you* know so much?" demanded Jasper, and Nutmeg smiled sadly.

"Hush, Lordling, or you will wake the child, and he will scream again. I cannot tell you how I know these things. I have been forbidden."

Jasper shrugged, and brushed past the old woman. She called after him, "I know which way you would use to leave the castle, Lordling, and you will find a boat for your use down in the harbour." She turned and walked away, then called softly, "Remember. In the Place of Dragons."

Jasper stared after her until Rosemary nudged him, and whispered, "Come on, let's go, otherwise your father's search-party will be ahead of us!"

Jasper grunted his agreement, and led the way down long, twisting, ill-lit corridors until he stood at the top of a flight of stairs which descended into darkness.

"We're well below ground level now, Rose. Count seventeen stairs, then stop, and wait."

Bravely, Rosemary stepped down into the dark, counting slowly. At seventeen, she halted, and waited for Jasper to catch up.

"Now," said his voice just behind her, "push with both hands at the wall on your right."

Rosemary did so, and a panel creaked back under the pressure, allowing a greenish glow to filter out on to the stairs. Quickly they slipped through the gap, and stood in a small round room, containing nothing but a deep well.

"Now comes the hard part, Rose. I'll have to lower you and the Shrimp down the well rope, and then slide down after you. There's an opening in the side of the well, and a tunnel which leads to the harbour."

The Shrimp woke as Jasper was letting the rope down the well, but he seemed reassured by the dank smell of water, and by Rosemary's nearness, so he made no sound. The rope descent slowed, then stopped, and Rosemary's eyes picked out a glowing stud in the wall. From below came a slight shush and slurp of water, but she put out a hand, hauled the bucket in which she and the Shrimp sat over to the wall, and then scrambled out into the low tunnel. The Shrimp came sure-footedly after her, and helped her hold the rope taut as Jasper came sliding down it, hand over hand.

They wasted no time now, but scrambled down the tunnel, following the mysteriously glowing studs. Jasper seemed to know his way well, and he did not halt until a fresh wind stirred the dead air of the passage, and the tang of rope and wood told them they were nearing the harbour.

Silently as a ghost, Jasper flitted ahead to make

sure that nothing lay in wait for them. It was just about sunrise by now, and the two children could see him creeping down to the bank of the Opal River. He took a good look round, especially at something the others couldn't see down below the bank, then came quietly back. He was frowning.

"How *could* she have known about this tunnel?" he muttered. "Only the Sards have ever used it, and we never speak about it."

"What is it?" asked Rosemary.

"You'd better come and see. I'd like to know what you think about it."

Rosemary and the Shrimp followed Jasper as he again crept out through the bushes which masked the tunnel exit, and led down to the bank. A little upstream of them stood the wharves and piers of the harbour, silent and deserted, but here in the deep water by the steep bank bobbed the most beautiful little craft that Rosemary had ever seen. It was shaped like a swan, with the bird's snowy head for a prow. The carved wings formed the sides of the boat, and the stumpy tail was the stern. It glowed with a starry light, as though more than just paint coloured it. The swan's head was crowned, and its eyes were deep blue. A canopy formed a shelter in the well of the boat, and there were three chairs waiting for occupants. No rope tied the boat to the shore. It just bobbed there on the current, waiting.

"Well, do we, or don't we?" asked Jasper.

Rosemary closed her mind and her senses to everything but the boat, trying to get the "feel" of it. "It's good," she announced. "Strange, but good."

"That's what I feel," replied Jasper, relieved, then chuckled to see the sleek, bewhiskered head of a seal pop out of the water by the swanship.

"The Shrimp's made up his mind already!" he

grinned, and stepped on board. Rosemary followed, and the seal flopped over the side too. Jasper and Rosemary pushed off from the bank while the Shrimp changed back.

"Where's Trout?" asked the little boy through the luxuriant moustache he had again forgotten.

"We had to leave him behind for a little while, at the castle. He'll be quite safe."

"Oh. Have we left my baby there too?"

"No. No, Shrimp dear. We've come looking for your baby. You must help us find it."

"How did it get lost?"

"Somebody took it. He won't hurt it, but your nasty man wants it, and if we don't find it, he might take it and hurt it. He might hurt the man who took it, too."

"Hawk-man? *He* might be hurt?"

"Yes, Shrimp. He might be hurt."

"Poor man. He hurts already. Here and here."

Jasper and Rosemary stared at each other. "Can he and Hawk be related?" said Jasper incredulously.

"That's the only way I can explain a shared feeling like that," agreed Rose. "Shrimp, is Hawk your father?"

The Shrimp looked frightened, and as usual avoided the awkward question. "Want Mamma!" he wailed, so they stopped questioning him.

Jasper was sitting in the stern, guiding the swanship by its steering oar, and when the Opal River forked on either side of a central island, he tried to steer down the left-hand channel, since it looked the calmer and deeper of the two. But though he leaned his whole weight on the oar, the ship carried on serenely sailing for the right-hand channel.

Rosemary looked round in alarm as shingle grated under the keel in the shallow channel, and she clung to the Shrimp as the ship bumped and

danced among tumbling rapids. Jasper's face was white with helplessness and fear; then, abruptly, the ship slid into deeper water, and the island and the channel were behind them.

Rosemary gave a squeak of alarm, and pointed back up the left-hand channel. Hidden from upstream by a bluff on the island, a black ship lurked at anchor, waiting to pounce on any boat trying to come down from the castle or the town.

"Do you . . . d'you think it belongs to the Night Raiders?" croaked Jasper.

"Must do," replied Rosemary, remembering her mother's words. "Princess Diana reported black ships sailing off the shores of Argentia—"

"And that's where the Opal River meets the sea."

Rosemary laid a hand in a stroking gesture on one of the wings of the swan. "Thank you, swanship. You obviously know where you're taking us, but I wish, oh, I *wish* you could tell us who you belong to, and who sent you."

The Shrimp wriggled round on his seat, his eyes very wide with surprise. "My Mamma's boat," he announced.

"But where *is* she, Shrimp?" asked Rosemary; then, even as the little boy's face crumpled, and he began to cry, she became so still that Jasper touched her, and said:

"Rose? Rose, what is it?"

The girl relaxed slowly, and said, her voice a thread of sound so faint the boy had to stoop to hear, "I think I've just had a brainstorm. I know where the Shrimp's mother is."

"What!"

"I do. I *do*!"

"You found my Mamma? Where?"

"*You* found her, I think, Shrimp."

"I did? How?"

"Now think. I'm going to ask you something, and you'll have to be really grown up, and think carefully about your answer. It's very important that you do answer, Shrimp."

The Shrimp was looking very anxious by now, so Rosemary said, "I'll hold your hands, Shrimp. Now. In Quarrine Castle, just after we got there, a serving woman came in, and you screamed. Why did you do that, Shrimp?"

"Acos she brushed something across my face, and it felt like my Mamma's feathers, but when I looked, it was an ugly old woman, an' I was frightened."

"Was it just the feathers that felt like Mamma?"

"No. She smelled like my Mamma too, all soft and fluffy, an' her eyes were blue an' twinkly, an', an' . . . oh! But it wasn't her, it wasn't, an' she's still lost!"

Excited by all the attention he was getting, but miserable too, the Shrimp was on the verge of tears. Rosemary put an arm round him, but spoke to Jasper.

"You remember when the Shrimp screamed?"

"Yes."

"Was Nutmeg anywhere near him? Did she touch him?"

Wordlessly, Jasper shook his head.

"Second clue. Who met us as we were leaving Quarrine Castle?"

"Nutmeg . . . who seemed to know which way I was going to take you out."

"Right, and what was waiting for us at the end of the tunnel?"

"The swanship!"

"Which the Shrimp . . . ?"

"Said belonged to his mother!" interrupted Jasper, his eyes glowing with excitement. His mind leapt ahead now, and he went on, "She's been at Quarrine Castle for about a year, and nobody knows where she came from."

"Has anyone ever asked her where she came from?"

"Yes, Mother asked her, but Nutmeg walked away as though she hadn't heard the question."

"She probably didn't hear it. Maybe it's a part of the same enchantment that's taken Hawk's memory away."

"I suppose that could be so . . . but what do we do now? Every moment that passes takes us further away from our one real clue in this tangle. We can't even land while we're following the river through these deep gorges in the mountains!"

"When do we get out of them?"

"Not until well after nightfall, at this rate of travel."

"Then we'll just have to be patient, won't we?"

"Hmmm. I'm not a very patient person by nature, Rose."

They were all glad when, at nightfall, the ship nosed into a little creek on an island in midstream. The children thankfully took the chance to stretch their legs among the bushes and flowers of the woody islet. A full moon was rising as they made their way back to the ship to sleep.

"I suppose we're into Argentia by now," said Rosemary, gazing at some white flowers growing nearby without really seeing them.

"Of course," replied Jasper. "I keep wondering how, in the name of the Powers, I can pass a warning on to Princess Diana, and Old Sol. I hate to think of them and Selena and Zonn, in danger from the Night Raiders."

"Full moon . . ." murmured Rosemary; then, with a muttered exclamation, she dropped to her knees beside the white flowers. "Jasper! D'you

know what these are?" she demanded excitedly. "They're moondaisies, and they open and turn their faces to the moonlight. Tonight, Princess Diana's Powers will be at their greatest . . . and I might be able to warn her, at least, and ask her to join us all at Mootmeet."

"It's worth a try! May I watch, or would you rather I went and sat with the Shrimp?"

"Oh, you know so much already, a little more won't matter," decided Rosemary, and sat back on her heels beside the flowers. Slowly, they turned their frail white petals to the moon, following its course across the sky. The girl began to sing, a cold, lonely, remote-sounding tune, without words. The flowers swayed and took on a glow of their own. From the moon came a clear, pure light, which bleached even the strongest colours to grey and silver, and stood every object beside its own duplicate in pearly shadow. Through this cold glow leapt one moonbeam whose light grew to the power of a searchlamp, and its radiance settled like a cone of mother-of-pearl over Jasper, the kneeling girl, and the moondaisies.

Down the moonbeam came walking, or gliding, a marvellously beautiful woman, with a fierce radiant face. Her robes were set in folds of silken sheen, and her long hair was wound round her head like a coronet.

"Who calls me from the sky, on the night of my Power?" she asked in a chilly voice.

"Rosemary Moschatel, Highness."

"You are far from the Arbour, child."

"Evil walks, Lady. I called to give a warning. The Night Raiders seek the Egg that sings. Why we don't know, but their leader, the Enchanter Doppel, is very powerful. Lord John Sard wants to call a Four-Family Council at Mootmeet to find a way to deal with him."

Princess Diana's face twisted into a smile, but it was so sad that it was more like weeping.

"I thank you for your warning, Rosemary. I know you meant well, but it is too late. I walk the night to seek my daughter. Doppel already has Selena, and I cannot find her. Old Sol keeps within doors at his mansion and rages because Zonn does not return home. I think Doppel does not have him yet, but he seeks him."

"Oh, no!" gasped Rosemary. The news was dismal, to say the least.

"A warning, children. Doppel feeds on Power. He has absorbed my daughter's. That's why I cannot sense where she is. He must be destroyed, I agree. I will come to Mootmeet, and I will bring Old Sol as soon as may be. Farewell. I will watch, from on high, as I search. Power be thine."

"And thine also," muttered Rosemary and Jasper together, automatically.

Princess Diana disappeared in a shimmer of moonglow, and the two children stared miserably at each other.

"She *must* be upset to speak so freely about Power!" remarked Jasper.

"She scares me. She's so cold and fierce!" murmured Rose.

"Selena's all right, though," suggested Jasper, "even if her tongue *is* a bit sharp at times. Poor girl. I wonder where she is?"

Quelling a spurt of jealousy, Rosemary asked quietly, "In the Place of Dragons? I have a strange feeling I'm going to hate that place. Are we near it?"

"Yes. Very, I'm afraid . . . if we go there. We'll decide in the morning."

"No. Now I'm sure that we should go there."

"Why this sudden reversal of feeling?"

"Because we know Nutmeg is fairly safe for the moment, with your father. Hawk, though, has the Eggchild, and it seems to be the key to this mystery."

"Very well. Now let's sleep, and don't you dare change your mind again!"

9

In the Place of Dragons

All the following morning the swanship sailed on
downstream, but in the mid-afternoon it drew
closer and closer to the bank, and finally drifted
into the mouth of a narrow creek. Rushes and
willows fringed the banks of the tributary, but the
swanship kept in the middle until the water
became so shallow that it could go no further.

"This is where we disembark, I think," said
Jasper, and leapt on to the bank. He helped
Rosemary out and lifted the Shrimp on to dry
land, even though the little boy kicked and wriggled.

"Want to go in the water! Leggo!"

"No, Shrimp, you're *not* going in the water.
We've got to walk now."

"Where?"

"To the Place of Dragons."

"What's a dragon?"

"It's a big scaly animal which can breathe out
fire if it wants to."

"Don't want to see one!"

"I'm afraid you may have to. You see, that's

where we'll find the Hawk-man and your baby."

"Oh. If baby's there, maybe I'll go."

All the time he was replying to the Shrimp's questions, Jasper was leading away from the creek towards the top of a low hill. Rosemary broke in anxiously. "D'you mean there really *are* dragons where we're going?"

"There weren't when I was there last, Rose, but it didn't get its name for nothing."

Rather relieved, Rosemary followed Jasper and the Shrimp in silence, until they reached the top of the hill. It was only from the crest that she realised just how high above sea level they were.

The land dropped sharply away below her, and far away ahead stretched Argentia, a flat land of still lakes and silver birch forests, among which flowed the great Opal River. On the edge of vision lay the sea, and the flashing towers of the Silver Palace. Much nearer to them, only about a mile away, rose the cracked and weather-crumbled walls of a natural, rocky amphitheatre. High cliffs surrounded a bowl of vivid grass, and a tiny lake. Shadows at the base of the cliffs suggested caves.

"That's the Place of Dragons," pointed Jasper.

Rosemary had been afraid it might be. "Is there only one way in?"

"Only one that I've ever seen. There's a break in the cliffs, about two horses wide, and you enter under an arch of rock."

"Are those caves I can see?"

"Yes. I suppose that's where the dragons used to live."

Rosemary was glad Jasper had said, "used to," but wasn't sure whether he'd said it just to give her courage.

"Tired!" wailed the Shrimp suddenly, and sat down heavily.

"We can rest a bit before going on, can't we?" begged Rosemary.

"No. We've got to get there as fast as possible and find out whether Hawk and the Eggchild really are there. Look." Rosemary followed Jasper's pointing finger with her eyes, and saw what he'd just noticed.

"Raiders?" Her throat was suddenly dry with fear.

"I think so. They've disguised their camp well, but who else would be camping out in the wilds of Argentia?"

"How far are they from the Place of Dragons, d'you reckon?"

"About two hours' ride. It's lucky we have the advantage of height, here, so that I noticed them. It's sheer luck if their scouts haven't found the Place of Dragons yet. We've got to beat them to it."

"But once in there, we'll be trapped!"

"We've got to risk that if we're going to make any attempt to get Hawk and the Eggchild out."

Wordlessly Rosemary nodded, hauled the Shrimp on to her back, and set off towards the cliffs.

It took them almost two hours to reach the entrance to the amphitheatre, because they had to take it in turns to carry the Shrimp, and it was tiring country for walking. At last, though, they stood at the foot of the rocks, and stared up at the great towers that wind and weather had worn into fantastic shapes.

"It's like a mountain with a hollowed-out middle," commented Rosemary, but Jasper just motioned her up and on to the rock arch which led into the Place of Dragons. The rock tunnel wasn't long, and soon they walked out on to soft grass and stopped, overawed by their surroundings. It was very, very quiet, and even the tiny laps of the wind-blown waves on the lake could be heard.

"Come on," encouraged Jasper. "We can see

they aren't out here. Let's go nearer the caves."

"Must we?"

"Don't turn coward now, Rose. You know we must find Hawk and the Eggchild."

"Shall I leave the Shrimp in the lake?"

"He'll be happiest in the water. Yes, I should."

Rosemary knelt down on the strip of sand beside the lake, told the Shrimp to be sure to come when she called, and watched him wriggle into the water and streak away like a speckled shadow as he turned into a trout.

"Now, I'm ready," she said, getting up and brushing the sand off her knees. She turned to find Jasper already walking towards the nearest openings in the cliffs, but even as she started to follow him, he turned back and stared at her.

"What's the matter?" she asked.

Jasper frowned, began, "Could we . . ." hesitated, then carried on, "I wonder whether we could save ourselves a lot of time by sounding these caves in one sweep rather than searching each individually?"

"I don't know what you mean by sounding."

Again Jasper hesitated, then said, "I've told you before that I can tell what the layers of rock below us are, remember? My family call the way we tell that sort of thing, 'sounding'. The thing is, I expect I could do it with holes in rocks above ground as well, but not by myself."

"You mean you could tell whether there was anything in them. Why don't we just call?"

"And bring any nearby Raiders down on us? No, thank you!"

Rosemary shuddered. "No. You're right. What would I have to do?"

"Simply turn me to face each cave, one after another. I'd have to concentrate so hard on the 'sounding' that I should be virtually blind and deaf to anything else."

"So I'd be just a direction-finder?"

"Yes."

"Let's do it, then."

Jasper stood still in the late afternoon warmth, his eyes shut, hands clenched, and body rigid as a bar of iron. Rosemary put her hands lightly on his shoulders.

Soundlessly, wordlessly, Power flowed from Jasper to the rocks, back again, and, through him, to Rosemary. Hands tingling, she turned him little by little until he had sounded all the visible caves, and some that she could not see at all, which must have been hidden by a sealing curtain of rock.

Only once was there a slight pause, when the boy retested one cave, and Rose noted carefully where it was, before moving on to the next. When they had finished, and Jasper was taking a rest by the lake, she walked over to the cave and peered into the gloom. It was not so much a cave as a deep gash in the rock, and inside Rosemary found a pile of sloughed dragon-skins, which crackled like old leather. The scent around them seemed very sharp and wild to belong to such old skins, and when she found a neat child-sized nest made among some stones further back, lined with leather, she instinctively bent to feel it. It seemed faintly warm to her touch, and a real, or imaginary, slither in the dark at the back of the cave sent her scurrying back out into the sunshine. Whatever she might have found, it certainly wasn't Hawk or the Eggchild.

Midway back to Jasper, still lying by the lake, Rosemary stopped, and tilted her head to listen. Really, her imagination must be working too hard. She thought she could hear . . .

"Rose, can you hear the same as me?" demanded Jasper huskily, grabbing her by the arm.

Eyes shining, they stared at each other, then turned to scan the cliffs of the Place of Dragons.

Soft and sweet, the Eggchild's song drew their eyes to the high rim of the amphitheatre. The children gasped with sheer pleasure. Sweeping gracefully down from the rocky towers came a lovely, reddish-brown pony, with slender legs, and vast wings which beat thunderously as it approached. On its back sat Hawk, cradling the Eggchild in his arms.

"Now we know what the 'son of the wind' is," said Jasper.

Together, he and Rosemary walked forward to meet Hawk as he dismounted. Anxiously, Rose noticed that his face was gaunter than ever, and yet he seemed stronger than he had been in Quarrine Castle.

Man and children stared at each other, then Rosemary ran forward to fling her arms round him. "I'm happy to see you," she said simply.

Hawk replied with a swift return hug, and by giving her the crooning Eggchild.

"I am healed, and as well as I can be," he said. "I seek for Doppel, but, now that it has made me well, I can't justify keeping the Egg that sings. When I saw you arrive, I took leave of the small friend I found here, and had Argamath carry me up to the crags to watch."

"Friend?" thought Rose, her mind pondering that little stony nest in the cave, but Jasper was looking at Argamath.

"Your horse?" he queried.

"Argamath, son of the wind," said Hawk, as the pony trotted forward to rest its head on his shoulder. The words were both a greeting and an introduction.

Rosemary was behind Hawk's back, frantically signalling to her cousin without making a sound. She was cupping her ear with one hand, and then pointing to the Eggchild. Suddenly he realised

what she wanted him to notice.

The Eggchild had fallen ominously silent.

Quickly Jasper grasped the situation. Here were Hawk—vulnerable, weaponless—and the Egg-child, which Doppel wanted. From the silence, it was more than likely that Raiders were close enough to present a danger.

Without a flicker of this flashing thought appearing on his face, Jasper made up his mind. Hawk had been talking, but the boy hadn't heard a word. He hoped he made sense when he spoke.

"Hawk, I know you want to find Doppel. The last place we heard of him was three hours' journey east of Quarrine Castle. That was yesterday morning, so he won't have moved that far since then."

Hawk looked somberly at the dark boy before him, and asked, "Why do you suddenly do this for me?"

"Because you put the Eggchild before your obsession with Doppel, and brought it to us. If you go to Quarrine Castle, I've no doubt my father will even give you a sword. Here. Show him this."

Jasper dragged a silver-set jasper-stone ring from his finger and gave it to Hawk, walked with him to the quietly grazing Argamath, and watched him mount. There was a feeling of oppression and danger in the air, to which Hawk seemed oblivious, but Jasper was not surprised to see Rosemary dart sideways to a tiny, half-hidden cave, and return without the Eggchild.

Hawk raised a hand in salute. "East of Quarrine Castle, you say?"

Jasper nodded, hiding his anxiety. Time was running out. He could feel the vibration of many hooves travelling through the rocks beneath his feet, and he began to despair of having time to send Hawk away, let alone hide Rosemary and himself.

"Go with Power," he said, and settled Hawk's departure by giving Argamath a hearty slap on the rump.

"Good luck, Hawk!" called Rose, as the winged horse leapt into the air, and flew over the shattered turrets and battlements of the rock opposite the red eye of the setting sun.

The cousins watched Hawk and Argamath go, barely holding themselves still, then sprang into movement. Both knew that their longest job would be to get the Shrimp out of the lake, so they ran to the beach, and began frantically slapping the water, and calling.

"It's no good," gasped Jasper. "We'll have to come back and get him when the Night Raiders have gone."

"You're sure they're coming here?"

"Aren't you?"

Rose didn't bother to reply directly.

"The Eggchild?"

"Get it. It'll be more at risk than the Shrimp, if we leave it here. They'll automatically search the caves if they're making camp. They're trained soldiers."

Rosemary turned to sprint across to the little cave, but it was already too late. She spun back again as Jasper gave a shout of alarm.

The thunder of hooves was suddenly all about them as mounted Raiders swirled in under the arch of the rock tunnel. The men's yells of triumph were deafening as they rounded up the two children like herd beasts. Jasper stamped, but nothing happened.

Silence, and stillness, came as Doppel himself, resplendent as ever, rode into the Place of Dragons, leading a packhorse with two childish figures draped over it, face down and tied on.

Horrified, Jasper and Rosemary could only stare at those unresponsive backs, and wonder. They couldn't see the heads.

Doppel didn't say a word. He simply pointed towards the lake, and rode majestically forward, twitching the reins of the packhorse.

Winded and half-stunned, Jasper and Rosemary were contemptuously flung over the saddles of their captors' horses, and taken to where Doppel had eventually dismounted.

The shadows were gathering in the rocky bowl as the silent men lit a fire by the lakeside, and dumped their captives in a row. Jasper and Rosemary had been securely tied, and now twelve-year-old Selena was dropped beside them in a tumble of silver-fair hair. In the fire-glow, they could see her face was black and blue, puffy with bruises. Finally, Zonn was flung down in a tangle of freckled limbs and shaggy red head. He moaned.

"He hit you?" gasped Jasper, staring at Selena.

"Almost every time I opened my mouth," agreed Selena.

"I wish I had more time to train you, you young vixen!" said Doppel as he came out of the shadows to stand and enjoy the terror, horror and impotent rage in the children's faces.

He seemed to be even more handsome than when they last saw him, and he looked taller too. Jasper remembered Princess Diana's words: "He feeds on Power," and shivered. He knew why he'd been unable to shock-wave the ground, as he had tried to do. The Enchanter was too strong now.

Doppel clapped his hands, and a Raider brought him a saddle to sit on, on the grass. Rosemary noticed that all around him the grass bent away from him, and turned brownish and dead-looking.

"Now, children," murmured Doppel silkily, "a few questions . . . No. That can wait awhile. First I will make sure you are harmless to me. Zonn, child of the Sun, your Power is already mine. Selena, Moon-daughter, I have drunk your quicksilver magic. But you two . . ."

Doppel turned his dark eyes on Jasper and Rosemary, and they wriggled, like butterflies impaled on a pin. "I do not know your Power, but it will be mine. Don't think you can outwit an Enchanter of my strength."

Doppel stared at Rosemary, and she closed her eyes, thinking hard of all the beautiful plants that were her care, slender lilies, dusky roses, yellow gorse, nasturtiums, mosses, grass; she thought of the strength of her trees, the honey smell of oak bark, the roughness of an elm, graceful willow and birch, resinous pine . . . but gradually her mental pictures turned into a chase, where she fled from a nameless terror down avenues of endless trees, not good ones but menacing, trees which reached out to tear and trip. She fought the terror, and found courage to stop, and turn to see it. She even waited, in that unreal battle, to see whether the great killer bear, the one that had killed her father, would attack her. Without weapons, she fought for all the things on which her Power depended: the natural strength of bulbs seeking the sun and spring rain, the regeneration of land after a blight, the rebirth of plants after long cold, the warmth of the rising sap; but, in turn, Doppel twisted her strength, and her gentle courage, and absorbed them. Desolately, Rosemary saw her Power in him as pestilence and poison, with spring after long winter. A well in herself which she had been unaware of was emptied, and she was left with nothing. Her mind spun away into darkness, but not before she had heard a satisfied chuckle from nearby.

Zonn and Selena had both fought and lost this kind of battle before Rosemary, and they wept as they saw her body slump, fainting, in its bonds.

Fury fed Jasper's strength to such an extent that, just for a moment, Doppel quailed when he turned his eyes on the boy. He realized his mistake in not tackling Jasper first. He had left out of account the depth of affection between Jasper and Rosemary, and he paid dearly for it.

"You will not do that to me!" swore Jasper, his eyes narrowed to slits of hatred and anger, and, fight as Doppel would, he could not suck out Jasper's Power. The boy took refuge in the strength of the steel, iron and adamant which were his concern in the Land of the Four Families. He could not afford to lose, because when rock breaks under stress, it shatters, and there is no mending it.

For an hour the man and boy struggled for mastery, and neither gained the victory.

At last Doppel turned to Rosemary, and snorted with impatience as he saw she was still unconscious. At his command, a Raider brought a bucketful of water from the lake, and emptied it over her. She spluttered and writhed, while the other three looked on in impotent rage.

Doppel started to question her, so Jasper kept interrupting, and drowning her answers when he saw she could not help but reply truthfully. Doppel put an end to this by gagging the boy, and he soon had the whole tale of their travels from her, including the whereabouts of the Eggchild. Strangely, just knowing where to find it seemed to satisfy him. He seemed curiously unwilling actually to lay hands on it, but his eyes gleamed when the Shrimp was mentioned.

"In the lake, you say?" he enquired softly, then turned to call. "Raiders, there seems to be a fish in the lake. Bring it to me for my supper, gutted and grilled."

Jasper thrashed in his bonds, but the ropes were tight, and seemed to cut in the more, the more he moved. Dopple's eyes narrowed.

"You hate to be helpless, don't you, boy? That's how Adler Windhover felt when he saw how I had broken the Power uniting his family."

The children watched in fascinated horror as the Enchanter's eyes grew opaque, and he seemed to go far away inside himself to savour some memory they felt sure he intended to make them share.

"All of them were there," began Doppel, and as he spoke, the air shivered, and the children seemed to look down into a mountain valley. Beside a river which gave off tendrils of steam stood a tall woman with silver-fair plaits wound round her head like a crown. She held the Shrimp by the hand, and her other arm cradled the Eggchild. She was laughing. Nearby, with his back to her, stood the man the children called 'Hawk,' patting a huge dragon on its head. "I came to the valley merely wanting the dragons there to reinforce my Raiders," said the Enchanter, "but I went away again doubled in strength." He chuckled at a private joke, and repeated, "Yes. Doubled."

The air shivered again, and the scene changed. The Enchanter stood by the stream, glaring fiercely down into the water, where a flicker of silver might have been the Shrimp darting away. Beside him on the grass bank lay the Eggchild, but, when he turned to pick it up, an aura of fire crackled around it. The Enchanter whirled round to face Hawk and the lady. Time passed, as a battle of invisible forces took place. The air twisted and shimmered, forming strange shapes and colours. The river boiled, and then froze, but all

the Power seemed to centre on the unmoving Eggchild. At last, however, Hawk stumbled and
swayed on his feet. The woman beside him swayed
too, as though her Power were united to his.

As suddenly as it had begun, the Enchanter's
memory-sharing halted. "I drained them, and I
drained you," he crowed. Then he tired of his
game of cat and mouse, and called two Raiders
over.

"Take these miserable creatures to a suitably
small cave. Put them all inside after checking for
any weapons. Then I'll cause a landslide to make
sure there is no escape. What never lives to grow
up can never be a problem to me. I shall enjoy
thinking of them slowly dying behind tons of rock
and rubble, and when I have the Eggchild, I will
have Power enough to sweep 'Hawk,' and their
beloved parents, into oblivion. I think *I* shall go to
this conference at Mootmeet, too. Yes. Mootmeet."

Jasper kept up a pretence of despair as ungentle
hands checked his clothes and found the knife at
his belt. More hands shoved him headfirst after
the three others into a little cave with a pool at the
back of it and, shortly afterwards, the shaking
rock, and the cloud of choking dust which bil-
lowed back into the cave, told him that the
Raiders had carried out their orders. A landslide
had cut off their light and air, and, it seemed, all
hope of a rescue.

10

Unexpected Help

When hope seemed lost, Jasper felt stronger than ever before, and he was even able to laugh when Selena muttered, "I'd have liked to give him a last tongue-lashing before I was bundled in here!"

She wriggled over in the darkness, and chewed off Jasper's gag.

"Aye, you've an acid enough tongue on you to wither even Doppel," gasped Jasper, and thanked her. Then he asked, "Rose? Are you all right?"

"I . . . I think so, Jasper. I'm just soaking wet and cold. If Doppel didn't draw off your Power, does that mean you can get us out of here?"

"If I were untied, yes, probably I could. Now I'm surrounded by stone, Doppel has no control over me. As it is, I can't do anything. Come on. Surely *one* of us can get free?"

For a while, the children wriggled and twisted in the darkness, trying to loosen their bonds, but one by one they had to stop to get their breath back.

"We've got to get out before morning," muttered Jasper. "He'll do just what he said: grab the Eggchild and go to Mootmeet."

There seemed to be nothing to say after this, until Selena asked, "Where was that place, where we saw the Eggchild and its parents?"

"No idea," growled Jasper, still angrily wriggling. He stopped, and considered. "Rose and I thought the Eggchild's mother was one of my father's servants."

"Obviously Hawk's *real* name is Adler Windhover, and that lady certainly wasn't a servant!" Selena snapped back.

"What is this Shrimp you kept speaking of?" asked Zonn, his voice blurred by a faint splashing from a pool at the back of the cave.

"Me," said a new voice. "I'm Shrimp. Who's that?"

"Shrimp?" called Jasper and Rosemary together. "You're not eaten!"

"Why should I be? No! Hello!" said the Shrimp in quick succession, and then added carefully, "Jus' a minute. I still got one fin, an' I want a foot instead."

Idiotically, the others began to gasp with laughter. The situation seemed so ridiculous. There were four of them tied up like chickens, while the little fifth one worried about changing a fin back into a foot.

Finally the Shrimp was pattering towards them, judging by the noise he was making. But he seemed to be talking to someone, or something, else.

"Come on," he said. "I can't see. You *said* you could breathe out fire. Well, I want to *see*."

"Oh all right," agreed a dry little voice. Suddenly, a small flame lit the darkness. The children caught a glimpse of each other's startled faces, and of something Jasper and Rosemary had failed to find all day.

"Shrimp, have you found Hawk's dragon?"

squeaked Rosemary. "I found his nest, and Hawk mentioned a 'friend' here. I wondered whether the friend was a dragon."

"Is you a dragon, Scruffy?" asked the surprised voice of the Shrimp.

"Course I am!" snorted Scruffy, producing more flame and a smell of burning.

"You told me dragons was big and scaly," said the Shrimp's voice accusingly.

"Well, I'm *little* and scaly," said Scruffy.

"Scruffy found me," explained the Shrimp. He had followed lots of underwater tunnels from the lake, but only one had seemed to go very far, and once in the caves, he had become confused, and got lost. Scruffy had heard him floundering around in a shallow tunnel, and had almost made the mistake of eating him before realising that the 'fish' he had caught now seemed to be human. Scruffy had taken to the water with the Shrimp, reluctantly, to show him the way out of the caves, and they had both surfaced in the small cave. Within the space of minutes, Scruffy and the Shrimp had the other children untied, and they rubbed each other's limbs to restore the circulation, careful not to mention the little blisters Scruffy had caused when he helpfully burned through some of the ropes.

"Now what?" asked Selena finally, and added, "All this burning's made the air in here even worse than it was. We're gradually using it up."

"I know," said Zonn. "How long d'you think it'll be before it gets too bad to breathe?"

"Judging from the accidents we sometimes have in the mines, we can last about half the night, and no more," warned Jasper.

"Well, that's long enough for Selena to get her Power back, then," said Zonn.

"What?" said Jasper and Rosemary together.

"Of course . . . Don't you know?"

"Know *what*?" demanded Jasper exasperatedly.

"That Selena and I can draw Power directly from the moon and the sun. It's night-time, so if she can only get a look at the moon, she can draw off its light and strength, and I thought, Jasper, since Doppel didn't drain you, you could get us out of here. Am I wrong?"

"No. I can get us out of here easily, now I'm untied. I've just been wondering whether it'd be a good idea to go thundering out through that landslide. Or should I bore a completely new exit? The Raiders could be watching to make sure we don't somehow manage to escape."

"Well, stop chattering and make up your mind!" snapped Selena. "I feel as wrung out as a piece of laundry, sitting here."

"My! You *are* feeling better, aren't you, sister dear!" mocked Zonn.

"Sister? Selena's your *sister*?"

"Oh I suppose you didn't know. Yes. She's my sister. It's a rule that sun and moon must never meet, so nobody's supposed to know that Old Sol and Princess Diana are married. I think it's mad, myself, but still . . . Anyway, when I was born they realized I was a sunchild, and I've always lived at Sunholm. When Selena arrived three years later, they decided she was a moonbaby, so that kept Princess Diana happy too."

"Chatterbox," muttered Zonn's sister, but he just chuckled. "Selena always sharpens her tongue on the people she likes best. She's really quite fond of me!"

He sounded so smug that even Rosemary began to feel happier and more cheerful, and she watched with interest as Jasper sat cross-legged in the glow which Scruffy produced, and clenched his fists, waving them in a set pattern round his head. Finally, his right arm pointed at a certain spot on the roof of the cave, and rock dust began showering down.

"What're you doing?" asked Zonn.

"Giving Selena a look at the moon," said Jasper curtly, and concentrated hard.

Rosemary leaned back against the walls of the cave, with one arm round the Shrimp, who had come crawling over to her for company. It was hard to avoid the damp patches on the rocks, but when she leaned back against a dry patch, she felt, as she put it later, "as if a spark ran through me to light a candle that had gone out." Power began to flow into her in a thin trickle, and into her mind's eye slid a picture of the patches of moss she had seen on the outside rocks that morning. She sat quietly, letting the generous moss pour energy into her, until she could sit up and say, "I'm going to do something about the air in here," and, to the surprise of the others, she began to sing. Immediately, their minds filled with pictures of spring: leaves bursting out of bud, bulbs pushing up from beneath winter-crumbled soil, and, as Rosemary sang, the moss spread, deepened, and ran fingers of green over the rock walls. It grew and grew, and produced strange, frail white flowers and bigger, different leaves which freshened the air as they released oxygen.

"Nice smell," said the Shrimp, snuggling closer to Rosemary and wriggling happily; and he dropped off to sleep, unaware that it was simply the difference between good and bad air that he had noticed.

The rock dust continued to swirl down from the narrow hole Jasper was boring, and the others followed the Shrimp's example until, as the first moonbeam fell on her face, Selena woke them all with a cry of pleasure.

Far, far above the roof of their cave, a small

hole opened to the sky, and down the hole poured the Power of the moon.

Scruffy was able to bank down his fire, which was making everybody uncomfortably hot, because soon they could all see by the radiance which glowed from Selena. As the moonlight fell on her, it was as though she were an empty glass which gradually filled with pearly white light, until her long fair hair swirled and crackled about her with an energy of its own.

"*Now* let him face me," she said fiercely. "When I've finished with him, he'll never say two sane words together again. I'll blast him with moon-madness, I'll . . ."

"Never mind that!" interrupted Zonn. "We all know what we'd like to do to him. What we need to decide is, what to do for the best now."

"Take the Eggchild to your parents at Moot-meet, as quickly as can be," suggested the rustly voice of the little dragon. "It must be protected if you are ever to release Lord Adler from his enchantment and destroy the man you call Doppel."

"We would if we had it . . ." began Jasper ruefully, but was interrupted.

"*I* got my baby," announced the Shrimp with smug importance.

Rosemary hugged him delightedly. "You clever boy!" she said. "Where have you put it?"

"Me 'n Scruffy took my baby away when you pushed it in that cave. It nearly fell down a hole!"

"Where is it now, Shrimp dear?" repeated Rose patiently.

"Scruffy gone to get it," said the little boy, and sure enough, only ripples on the black water at the back of the cave showed where Scruffy must have gone. He was soon back, cradling the Eggchild between the little wings on his shoulders.

By the Eggchild's golden light, Rosemary saw

Scruffy clearly for the first time.

"What beautiful bronze scales!" she exclaimed, then added, "Scruffy, you called Hawk by that other name."

"Lord Adler," nodded Scruffy.

"Do you know him well then?" asked Jasper.

"Of course I do," hissed Scruffy. "Every self-respecting dragon does. He is the head of the family which cares for all animals. But his special concern is for dragons, eagles, and the sons of the wind."

"What *are* these sons of the wind?" asked Zonn.

"Flying horses, of course," said Scruffy irritably. "For children of Powerful Families, you're awfully ignorant!"

"Is Hawk . . . I mean, Lord Adler, the father of the Eggchild?"

"Naturally. Doppel alone knows what happened to Lady Swanilda, though."

"The Eggchild's mother?"

"Yes. A very beautiful lady. She looked after the birds. The Shrimp there"—Scruffy pointed a claw at the little boy—"is Lord Adler's only son. The poor child's been on his own now for a year or so."

"I suppose he survived by spending most of his time in the streams and lakes. But I'd no idea there was a fifth family who cared for the animals. It's what we've needed for years!"

"Madam-mother said that, only the day before I left home. We've got a plague of deer in the Arbour . . ."

"Oh, shut up!" said Selena rudely. "What was it you said about getting the Eggchild to Mootmeet?"

"Get the Eggchild to safety. The child there tells me you think you've found his mother," said

Scruffy. "If so, release her first, and she and the Eggchild will call Lord Adler to them. Wherever he is, Doppel will not be far away."

"Well," faltered Rose, "we *thought* we'd found the Shrimp's mother, but after what you've just said and we saw, I'm not so sure. Nutmeg's no beauty."

Scruffy snorted smoke. "She won't look beautiful under enchantment! Probably quite the opposite. If you release her, and have the Eggchild, there will be real hope for Lord Adler in the last battle."

"Before we go, Scruffy, can you tell us why the Eggchild is so vitally important? I know it's Powerful, because I can feel it refilling me now, but that can't be all."

Scruffy scratched behind his left ear with a claw while he thought, then said, "As far as I know it, the story is this. The Windhover family lived in their valley in the really high ice-peaks, far to the south-west of here, beyond Quarrine."

"Wasn't it awfully cold?" asked Zonn. He liked heat. The hotter it was, the better it suited him.

"No!" snorted Scruffy. "The valley is deep, and it's kept very warm by hot springs which bubble up in the caverns. The ice peaks and their caves were above and all around, but they were very snug in their valley."

The children looked at each other, and Rosemary said, "That explains the steam rising from the river!"

"Quite possibly," nodded Scruffy. "How did you know that, though?"

Jasper explained briefly what the Enchanter had shown them of his encounter with the Windhover family. Scruffy snorted. "What you saw was part truth," he admitted, "but it was distorted."

"What really happened, then?" asked Zonn.

"Even I can't tell you a full story," said the little dragon. "What I know is this. A man came to the valley. He said his name was Ilkar Yumal. He had heard of the dragons, but not of Lord Adler and his family."

"So he didn't expect the dragons to be cared for and protected!" exclaimed Zonn.

"Precisely. He wanted them, because he knew that he was powerful enough to control them and mould them into a fighting unit to back up his Raiders when he attacked the Country of the Four Families."

Even Selena shuddered at the thought of spell-bound dragons shrivelling everything in their path. Scruffy continued sadly, "Lord Adler and the Enchanter are both proud men, and they made the same mistake of underestimating each other's strength. At that stage, the Enchanter could have been overthrown by Lord Adler and his wife, except for one thing."

"The Eggchild?"

"Yes. I don't know the secret of the Eggchild, but the Enchanter felt its Power. He knew that if he drained the Eggchild, he could overcome its parents, so he stole it."

"He didn't drain it, though, so what went wrong?" asked Selena.

"First of all, Lord Adler and Lady Swanilda set their son beyond the Enchanter's reach."

"In the stream?" asked Rosemary, remembering Doppel's glare as he watched the water, knowing he had no control over it.

Scruffy nodded. "When he was safe, they tried to rescue the Eggchild, and when they found they could not before he drained and killed it, they deliberately weakened themselves by dividing their Power in order to protect it from all harm. In this weakened state, Lord Adler was robbed of his memory and identity, so that, by stages, his Power would feed the Enchanter. My Lord was doomed to wander, forever following the Enchanter, hoping to kill him and regain his memory.

"That's been puzzling me," confessed Jasper. "Hawk said once or twice that he'd killed the Enchanter, but he obviously hadn't."

"You're wrong. He had," said Scruffy, "but it is all a part of the enchantment. Every time the two men fight, my Lord loses more Power as energy drains from him to his opponent, and, even though my Lord is the better swordsman, and appears to win the fight, no ordinary sword can kill the Enchanter now. He becomes more and more like Lord Adler. That's why he began to call himself Doppel. It's the Raider way of saying 'double.' "

"But that *still* doesn't tell us why the Eggchild is so important!" exclaimed Zonn. "There must be something else about it that nobody but its parents and Ilkar Yumal know about."

"I agree," said Jasper, but added harshly, "We're wasting time, now. We need to go while it's still dark. Is the Eggchild helping you at all, Zonn?"

"Yes. I'll be all right until the sun rises, and soon after that I'll be back to full Power."

"Good. Let's go, then. It's my belief that Doppel won't wait around here once he's sure he's had all the caves searched. He'll wait till morning, carry out a thorough search, then ride for Mootmeet in a fury. He'll be mounted, while we'll be on foot, but we must still get there first."

He swung round to Zonn and Selena. "Who're we likely to find at the mansion?"

"Mr. Sereleaf, in his beloved library!" laughed Zonn, but when Jasper glared at him, he thought seriously for a moment. "My father and Princess Diana won't be there yet. Whether the Sards and Lady Fenella will have arrived, I'm not certain."

"A pity, if not," murmured Jasper, then turned to face the wall. Again chips, dust and lumps of rock began to fall and, gradually, Jasper walked forward into the tunnel he was creating. The others followed him out, and enjoyed deep breaths of fresh air when they stood once more amidst waist-high grass and bushes.

Scruffy stuck his nose outside to look around, but soon retreated. From just inside the tunnel, he called huskily, "You'll need to combine Power to release Lady Swanilda, and your parents won't like that. Be deciding what you feel about it yourselves, on your way to Mootmeet. Goodbye."

Before the children even had time to turn and whisper their thanks, he was gone.

"Fast as we can without collapsing, now," said Jasper grimly. "Zonn, you and I will have to take turns giving the Shrimp a lift, so we'll have to leave the Eggchild to the girls."

"Stop organizing us, and get moving!" snapped Selena, and led the way downslope. Zonn chuckled as he followed her. The other three came in a group at the rear, Jasper angry, Rose cradling the Eggchild, and the Shrimp yawning.

11

Race to Mootmeet

❧

By midmorning, the children knew that they were
beaten. None of them had any energy left except
Jasper, the only one who had not succumbed at all
to the Enchanter. The others moved more and
more slowly. Zonn took progressively shorter
turns helping the Shrimp along, and the two girls
were finding the Eggchild a heavy burden. The
one who was carrying it felt well and strong, but as
soon as she handed over to the other, she became
deadly tired.

Finally, Jasper called a halt, and they all sank
down, propping their backs against the silver
birches which made up the forests of Argentia,
through which they were travelling. For a few
minutes there was quiet, except for birdsong and
the Eggchild's soft crooning.

"What are we going to do?" asked Zonn, at
last. He was looking anxiously at his sister.

Although she'd been very brave about it, Selena
had suffered the worst at Doppel's hands, because
of her biting tongue. The Enchanter had not been

gentle with his blows, and she was black and blue. As the Eggchild did its healing work, her face gradually became its normal size and shape, but she was still battered to the point of collapse.

"I don't . . ." began Jasper, then said, "Listen!" He held up one hand commandingly. Immediately, the others heard it too—the sound of many hoofbeats.

"Raiders!" hissed Zonn, and looked round for shelter.

"It can't be!" contradicted Rose.

"Why not?"

"Because the Eggchild's singing loudly."

"That's true," exclaimed Jasper. "It goes absolutely quiet when the Raiders are nearby. It's a sure warning."

"Who can it be, then?" asked Selena languidly. She was so tired, she didn't really care.

Jasper was thinking quickly. "Under the bracken, everybody," he snapped, and growled at Rose when she raised her eyebrows, "I'm getting cautious in my old age. I'd rather see these horsemen before they see me, Eggchild or no Eggchild."

Rosemary shrugged, and joined the others in the camouflaging shelter of a dense carpet of shoulder-high bracken.

She wasn't there long. At first glimpse of the riders through the trees, she was on her feet and running straight into her mother's arms. Ten minutes of uproar ensued as the cavalcade arrived.

"How did you find us?" asked Jasper.

Lord John pointed at the Eggchild. "Our horses gave us no choice. We were still keeping a look out for those Raiders as we made our way to Moot-meet. Suddenly, our mounts decided for themselves that we were going in the wrong direction, and they wouldn't respond to rein or voice. They brought us here, and stopped.''

"I'm glad they did!" exclaimed Rosemary.

"So am I," agreed Lady Fenella, who still had an arm round her daughter, as though she was afraid Rosemary might rush off again at any minute. "How do *you* come to be here, though? And with Selena and Zonn?"

Jasper turned to look at his father. "I'm sorry we left the Castle the way we did, Father. We had good reasons, believe me, but please don't let's waste any time here now. We'll tell you everything that's happened as we ride."

"What is the urgency, my son?"

"Doppel is also riding to Mootmeet."

"Here then is real need for haste. Mount up, and ride. Don't spare the horses!" called Lord John to his soldiers. Within seconds Selena and Zonn had doubled up with soldiers, while Jasper mounted behind his father and Rosemary in front of her mother. Lady Amethyst managed the Eggchild and the Shrimp.

As they rode, the children told the tale of their adventures, and since the adults kept interrupting with questions, it took them most of the long ride to Mootmeet to finish the story. The shadows were growing long as the cavalcade left the forests behind it, and the weary horses trotted up the long slope to the high walls of Mootmeet. Servants had been sent ahead from Quarrine to warn those at the great mansion that the Families would be arriving soon, so rooms were prepared and ready.

Lord John's first orders were for the great gates to be closed and barred to all comers except Old Sol and Princess Diana, who had not yet arrived, and for his own soldiers to organize a patrol rota for the walls. Lady Amethyst took the Shrimp and

Selena, and put them to bed straight away. Nobody could ever remember having seen Selena so quiet and docile before, so they all realized how ill she must be feeling.

The other children were allowed to stay up, and hear the parents' news while they all ate a very welcome hot meal. But it almost began with an argument. Lord John was not at all anxious to explain what he termed 'adult concerns' to the children, and tried to change the subject but Jasper was adamant.

"We 'youngsters,' as you call us, are the ones who've suffered most at the Enchanter's hands, so far! You only know of his Power by hearsay. *We've* experienced it. Don't try and tell Selena her face doesn't hurt, or Zonn and Rosemary that it wasn't terrifying to be totally bereft of Power. Yes, I said *Power*! . . ." By now, Jasper was really furious, face red with rage, and black hair standing out from his head like a wire brush. His father stopped him, and, surprisingly, he wasn't angry.

"I'm sorry, Jasper. I owe you an apology. I forget that you're sixteen, and Zonn's fifteen. Very well, the things that are worrying us are as follows. Princess Diana and Old Sol, who should arrive here early tomorrow, told us of the disappearance of Selena and Zonn. Doppel attempted to blackmail Princess Diana into helping him, but she refused. That was when we all realized just what a dangerous threat he was to us all, and to the peace of our country."

"Coastal trade from Argentia is at a standstill," added Lady Fenella, "because there are Raider ships waiting to pounce on any merchantman foolish, or brave, enough to put to sea, and they are merciless to their prey. They take no prisoners. That was why we were so fearful for you children, until we realized that Doppel knew of your Power, and wanted it for himself.''

"As we see it, though," went on Lord John, "many of our questions have been answered by what you have told us of the man you call Lord Adler. It was simply his misfortune that the Enchanter heard of the dragons under his control, and wanted them himself."

Jasper nodded vigorously in agreement, but his face fell again as Lady Fenella spoke.

"It seems to me," she said, "that if Lord Adler had not hidden the Eggchild at the Arbour, we should never have realized that we were under attack until it was too late. What really worries me, though, is, it may seem to you, a rather selfish thing. Why did Ilkar choose to attack the Windhover family first? What is the extent of their Power, and could it threaten us?"

The children gasped, then were silent at a frown from Jasper. He saw that their parents were tired and worried, and this was not the time to start trying to make them realize their misunderstanding. His own father seemed to have the best grasp of the situation, and all the children felt a little better when Lord John said, "Regardless of our different opinions, Fenella—and, remember, we haven't heard from Old Sol and Princess Diana yet—we *must* not precipitate a crisis."

"I agree," said his wife and Lady Fenella together, and all the adults looked sternly at their independent-minded offspring.

"The formality and ritual of Council Meetings at Mootmeet extend to you children *as well*," warned Lord John. "Don't do anything without Four Family agreement."

At a wink from Jasper, Rosemary obligingly yawned loudly, said, "Excuse me, I'm tired," and drew everyone's attention. Lady Fenella declared that it was way past bedtime anyway, and the children were soon in bed in the nursery wing of the house, with the Eggchild glowing and chirruping happily in the girls' room.

By the time they got up the following morning, Princess Diana and Old Sol had arrived, closely pursued by Doppel and the Raiders, and all the adults had closeted themselves in the Great Council Chamber to discuss the situation. Mootmeet was, to all intents and purposes, besieged; yet, so far, Doppel had made no demands or threats.

Lessons were arranged with Mr. Longthorn, the Sard family tutor, but they were often interrupted, since, one by one, the children were summoned to the great Council Room, where the parents sat and questioned them on all they knew, or could guess, about the Windhovers. As the day went on, the children who were called out for their turn of cross-examination came back looking glummer and glummer.

Jasper was the last to be called, long after schooling had finished for the day, and he came back to the nursery wing looking really tired and depressed. All the others except the Shrimp, who had gone to bed earlier, were waiting for him in what had been the playroom. The toys were still there, draped in white cloths to keep them clean, since they were so rarely used, and there was only one flickering light in the room. The Eggchild lay in an old doll's cradle, making its own pool of golden light, and crooning softly to itself.

Jasper came in, and shut the door wearily behind him. He looked round silently at the young faces gazing up at him, and shrugged. Then he sat down, without a word to say.

"You think what we do," finally suggested

Zonn. Jasper shook his head hopelessly, as if trying to shake away the flickering shadows.

"I don't know *what* to think," he said at last. "I couldn't make them understand the way we see what's been happening, and I couldn't follow their reasoning either. It was as if we were talking different languages. They want to go *slowly*—and they didn't believe me when I tried to explain that Doppel isn't reasonable, and that he moves like lightning."

Selena looked up and said sharply, "They're scared."

"What of?" demanded Rosemary.

"The Windhovers' Power, of course."

"She's right, you know, Rose," agreed Jasper quietly. "When you think about it, everything we've told our people about Lord Adler and the Shrimp points to the fact that they've got a lot of Power—quite as much as we have—and it's of a rather different kind."

"That's true," agreed Rosemary, "and yet the Sards met Lord Adler, when we brought him to the castle, and both Lord John and Lady Amethyst liked him."

"That doesn't make any difference; all our parents have the good of the whole country in mind, and they'll put that before any personal likes and dislikes," said Zonn, and Jasper backed him up.

"We wouldn't want them to do anything else, would we? But the trouble is, we're convinced that the land of the Four Families would be better off, and safer, with the added Power and protection of the Windhovers. What we've got to do somehow is to convince our parents."

"Has it occurred to anyone that the Windhovers may not *want* to settle here?" asked

Selena tartly. "We're busy planning a future which may not fit in at all with what Lord Adler will want, if we can free him."

"We're not completely stupid, Selena!" Jasper snapped back. "Of course we've thought about that possibility. But I'd like the Windhovers to be able to settle in our country if they choose. Just think of all the things Lord Adler and the Shrimp could help with. For a start, they could keep away the silly basilisks which pester our miners . . ."

"They could stop the plague of deer in the Arbour, and keep the horrid bears away . . ."

"We've got squirrel-trouble in the new pine plantation at Sunholm . . ."

"Mother was saying the shoals aren't coming inshore this year, and the fishermen are worried. Maybe the Shrimp could . . ."

"There you are!" said Jasper triumphantly. "We've all thought of ways they could help us, even you, Selena."

"I do *hope* we can help Lord Adler," said Rosemary wistfully. "He's so bereft of everything, and the Shrimp misses his parents, especially his mother."

Jasper peered in concern at his young cousin. Beneath what she had just said lay the things she remembered, but had never spoken of to anyone but Corrie, about the death of her father, Lord Peter. Jasper opened his mouth to say something comforting, but never said it, because suddenly, the glow from the Eggchild increased, and it crooned loudly. But it was only old Nutmeg who came into the playroom, carrying a tray of hot milk drinks and biscuits.

"Time for bed," she told them, and waited to carry away the empty mugs.

When she had gone, Rosemary turned to

Jasper, and said, "Nutmeg's our *only* clue. I've just had an idea about that. Remember what Scruffy said? 'Release her first, and she and the Eggchild will call Lord Adler.' While you tell the other two what we know about her, I'm going to the library, because I need to look through the Council Records. D'*you* have to learn them too?"

"Of course. We all do, as part of our education. I've got as far back as the time of . . . now, who were the Heads-of-Family? . . . Lord Onyx, Lord Valerian, Lady Ashtoreth, and Lord Zonn."

"You're much further back than I am, then. How far do the Records go?"

"Back about a thousand years, I think."

"More than that . . ." began Zonn, but Rosemary had gone.

12

The Net

❧

In fact, when Rosemary consulted the Librarian, Mr. Sereleaf, she found that the records went much further back.

"Where do you want to start, young lady?" enquired the Librarian helpfully, delighted to find someone young and interested to talk to.

"It's very important I find out all I can about Enchanters," said Rosemary, looking hopefully around the huge room.

Mr. Sereleaf's eyebrows shot up to his hairline, and his spectacles slid to the end of his nose.

"Oh dear! Oh dear me! That's a very, *very* old book you'll be wanting then. There're only two which will be of use to you. You will be careful with them, won't you?" And still muttering, "Oh, dearie dear," under his breath, Mr. Sereleaf dragged some tall library steps to a bookcase, climbed to the top, and searched along a row until he pulled out the two volumes he was looking for.

Reluctantly, he handed them down to Rosemary, who took them over to a reading table and lit the lamp there.

When Mr. Sereleaf came over to say, "You will call me if you're having any trouble, won't you? I can't read them myself, but I should be able to break your concentration if the words hold you spell-bound." Rosemary was already leafing through the first book and she understood what he meant. These books had been written by someone who had great personal Power, which had been communicated in the writing. Sometimes, the strange words of incantations moved under her eyes, and she had to exercise her own Power to make them stay still. With some, this worked. With others, it didn't, and Rosemary felt with increasing despair that the story, or the incantation, she could not read might be the very one which could free Lady Swanilda.

Then, when her eyes were smarting from the concentration, she found a story which seemed to leap out of the page at her.

"In the days of the Great Council came a man from Flammersea, who called himself the Enchanter. He had Power, of a kind, but it was of little strength to match his ambition. Lord Simon Hemlock fell to one of his spells, however, before we of the other three Families could convene to overthrow the upstart. At Mootmeet we held the Great Council, and I, as the chosen, devised his release. The symptoms of the enchantment were loss of memory, inability to speak of himself, and a strange change of appearance, while retaining his characteristics. Lord Simon appeared a youth in years, yet spoke with the authority of his maturity, he being at this time of forty years.

"For his release, I brought to him an object of innocent Power, which had done no wrong, and which could not tolerate the existence of evil. Lord Simon, when the Power object was put into his arms, became himself again, but had to be restrained for a short while until the readjustment to his normal appearance and manner took place. If he had been allowed to go during this time, I am certain he would have wandered forever insane."

Rosemary re-read the story, then carefully shut the book. Barely able to contain her excitement, she thanked Mr. Sereleaf for his help, and ran all the way back to the playroom. It was very late by now, so she planted a kiss on the unresponsive shell of the Eggchild, hurried into the girls' bedroom, and just had time to undress and scramble into bed before their parents looked in on their own way to rest. Surprisingly, she slept well, but was up early to announce, "I think we can free the Shrimp's mother, between us, if we try."

A babble of questions broke from the others, but it was the Shrimp's cry which was heard.

"Where is she? Where's my Mamma?"

Rosemary knelt in front of the little boy, and the room was quiet as the others all waited to hear her reply.

"You and the Eggchild have found her, I think, Shrimp, and between us, we can set her free. Listen."

Rosemary recounted the story she had found among the old Records, and ended, "So they *must* have combined Power in olden days. If they could do it before, why can't we now?"

"Mainly, I suppose, because we no longer know what each Family can do," suggested Zonn. The corners of his mouth crept upwards as he pictured his sister explaining her moon-magic.

"Are you suggesting we combine Power now to free Lady Swanilda?" demanded Selena frostily.

"Yes, I am."

"And what if it's all a mistake? What if Nutmeg is really what she seems, just a harmless old woman?"

"Do you really believe that, Selena?" asked Jasper.

"You've seen the way she avoids the Eggchild, and the Shrimp," added Zonn. "After what Jasper told us last night—the Shrimp's reaction in the castle, Nutmeg's advice about Hawk, *and* the swanship—can you really doubt that she's Swanilda, under Enchantment?"

Selena stared coldly for a moment, then dropped her eyes before Zonn's glare, and shrugged. "No. I suppose not." She returned immediately to the attack, though, asking, "Did you tell our parents all this when they called you into the Council Chamber?"

"Would *you* have done?" demanded Zonn irritably. "We didn't know then all we do now, anyway—and besides, how would they have reacted? 'We must not precipitate a crisis.' "

Jasper frowned and said, "Careful how you speak about my father, Zonn. So far, he's been right in his treatment of the situation."

"True," agreed Zonn, "but how long can we afford to leave sources of vital information out of reach?"

"Oh, stop it!" exclaimed Selena. "You're beginning to talk like Father. 'Sources of vital information' indeed! I suppose you mean Nutmeg?"

"Lady Swanilda, yes," snapped Zonn.

"What do you think she can tell us, that's vital?" demanded Selena.

"How to call Lord Adler here, for a start. *And* she can tell us why the Eggchild's so important," said Rosemary's quiet voice. Silence fell. At last, Selena nodded, and Jasper, as the eldest, began what had to be done.

"We must know each other's Power," he stated. "In a way even our parents do not know

each other's Power." The others nodded solemnly. "My Power is in knowing the metals, gems
and minerals of the ground beneath without the
need to see. I feel the slow movement of the liquid
interior of the earth, and I can make the ground
shake, and the great rocks tremble and move, far
beneath the earth."

His deep voice ceased, and there was a momentary silence. Rosemary felt quite overawed, and
shaken, until Jasper, catching sight of her face,
smiled and winked at her. The wink changed him
back from a frightening and powerful person to
the cousin she had known and loved all her life.

Selena spoke next, and she suddenly seemed
older, remote as the moon, as she blinked her
silver-glinting eyes and said, "Mine is the Power
of the moon over tides in the oceans and in humans. I can call on the power of the waves to
create storm and wind, I can bring lashing cold
rain, or limpid mild weather. I can strike beasts
and men with moon-madness, make land barren
or fertile. With a bow, I cannot miss the mark,
however distant. Silver is my colour, and my
metal, and white beasts are my care."

"Corrie and I between us make sure we all eat,"
said Rosemary. "Within a week, we could turn the
whole country into a desert where weeds would
choke weeds, and nothing wholesome would
grow. All plants and trees are our care. That's
all."

"All? That's enough, isn't it?" laughed Selena,
surprisingly. "Now you, brother," she urged
Zonn.

"I can summon day-weather of any kind which
is governable by the sun. I can blister and burn to
ashes, or shine mildly on all plants, beasts and
men. I can control the hot things of this world,
volcanoes, and molten metals. Gold is my metal,

and my colour, the bow and lance my weapons. Smiths and those who work with fire and metal are my brothers in spirit.''

Again there was silence.

''Well!'' sighed Jasper at last, looking round at the others. ''Now what?''

''We're completely interdependent in Power!'' exclaimed Rosemary. ''So we can go ahead, if we want to.''

''What's our object of innocent Power going to be?'' asked Zonn.

''The Eggchild, idiot!'' snapped his sister, and went on, ''How are we going to restrain Swanilda if we succeed in breaking the enchantment? Or are we going to wait for our parents?''

They looked at each other.

''*Are* we precipitating a crisis?'' asked Rosemary anxiously.

''Quite possibly,'' said Jasper, his voice hard.

''Jasper, what *did* you say to your father in the Council Chamber?'' asked Rosemary.

''I told him enough of what I thought of his spinelessness to make him forbid me, under oath, to do anything without a Four-Family agreement.''

''That settles the question then, doesn't it?'' sighed Zonn.

''Does it?'' demanded Jasper. ''Who will be making Four-Family decisions in thirty years' time?''

He looked round the circle of eager faces, and watched understanding come.

''*We* are the future decision-makers. In answer to your original question, Selena, no, we are not going to wait for our parents. Rose and I began this adventure, and we'll end it. Lady Swanilda deserves to be freed, if only to comfort the Shrimp, and when she has called Lord Adler here,

it may help him in the last fight if his wife is free,
and giving us aid against Doppel.''

Rose suddenly looked scared. ''You've decided
I'm right, have you? What if we're wrong?''

''If we're wrong, Rose, asking Nutmeg to hold
the Eggchild can't do any harm. She always avoids
it carefully when she brings us our meals. No. I'm
sure you're right.''

''If it works, do you . . .''

''*When* it works, what?''

''*When* it works, do you think she'll be a
human, or a swan?''

There was silence, then Selena said slowly,
''That's a good thought. I've noticed that in a
crisis the Shrimp looks for the nearest water. I'd
say she'd reappear as a swan, if her name is to be
believed.''

The others agreed, and they decided that the
best way of restraining a swan was in a net.

''Let's try to make a net, then, woven from all
our Powers, to rescue Lady Swanilda,'' suggested
Jasper.

''Me too?''

''Yes, Shrimp, you especially, because she's
your Mamma.''

The children sat down in a wide circle. Rosemary fetched a strand of creeper from the wall
outside the window and put that in the centre of
the circle.

As her hands wove through the air, so the
strand of creeper grew and crossed, until a mesh
net lay tumbled on the floor. Next, Selena and
Zonn sang into being the weights of warm gold
and cool silver all around the edge of the net.
Jasper sent a strand of light steel through every
strand of the net, and with extreme concentration,
and a lot of face-pulling, the Shrimp hung a
border of tiny iridescent fish scales from every

knotted square. It was finished.

"Isn't we clever?" sighed the Shrimp. The other four looked on in silence, the same question in all their minds. The net was certainly beautiful, but would it work?

"Who's going to fetch her?"

"Don't have to. Ring the bell, and she'll come."

Zonn was the only one who moved, and he took a deep breath before jerking the rope which would ring the bell far below in the servants' quarters.

As the Eggchild's song grew louder they knew that Nutmeg must be approaching. Finally the song reached a high note, and then the Eggchild stopped, so that the light tap on the door was clearly heard by all.

"Come in," called Jasper, and Nutmeg hobbled in, bent and withered, and crippled with rheumatism.

She looked round, her blue eyes twinkling, and said, "Did you want something, children?"

None of them quite knew how to answer, but suddenly the Shrimp burst out, "We think you're my Mamma but you can't tell us 'cos you're enchanted, so we is"—he looked at Rosemary—"we *are* going to set you free."

Nutmeg smiled again, looking at the shining net on the floor. "Are you going fishing to catch a Nutmeg?" she asked, as though she had not heard a word the Shrimp had said.

"In a way, yes," said Zonn, grinning sunnily back. "We've made a net of Power, you see, so we can't ask you to help us lift it, but you could hold the Eggchild for us as we go downstairs. It'll save us running all the way back up to fetch it."

"That was pretty good, on the spur of the moment!" muttered Selena, looking in surprised admiration at her brother.

Nutmeg began to protest, "I'm sure you can manage . . ." and all at once, her eyes were anxious.

"Pick up the Eggchild, Nutmeg!" ordered Jasper.

The old woman hobbled reluctantly over to the doll's cradle, then hung back fearfully. Quickly, the children bent and grasped the net around its edges.

"Pick it up," repeated Jasper remorselessly, and Nutmeg bent and did as she was bidden. The Eggchild shrieked, and the glow from it lit the whole room.

The adults approaching along the nursery wing corridor broke into a run, and when they rushed into the playroom, it did look as though some disaster had occurred.

Rosemary, sobbing, was putting the Eggchild back in its cradle. The other children struggled to hold down a sparkling net over something which thrashed wide wings and writhed like a mad creature; but even as the adults leapt forward to help, the Eggchild's voice rose above the pandemonium and the great bird quietened, and stopped stabbing through the net with its beak.

As the children relaxed, the Shrimp wriggled under the net like an eel, and began flinging it off. The heavy folds fell away, and uncovered a beautiful woman lying on the floor. Long silver-fair plaits framed her face, and when she slowly opened her eyes, they were still Nutmeg's, dark-blue and sparkling.

Expectantly, the children watched her get to her feet, and waited for her to speak. She gazed round at the roomful of people, but seemed to notice nobody but the Eggchild. She picked up the glowing, crooning bundle, and turned to the open window.

"It's almost finished," she whispered. "Egg-child, my child, call your father. If we are ever to be completely free, it must be ended now."

The adults, meanwhile, broke into speech.

"How *dare* you face me, oath-breaker!" rumbled Lord John, sending shudders through the floor from his tapping foot.

Jasper's protest was drowned by Old Sol's roar of disapproval at his own son, through which cut Princess Diana's icy voice, "And what is *your* explanation, daughter?"

Lady Fenella just looked, but to Rosemary, it was as though she was suddenly the rankest weed that ever grew, and she blushed scarlet.

A new voice brought immediate quiet. Lady Swanilda turned back from the window, and spoke directly to Lord John. "The enemy is outside the gates, and his opponent, who must champion all of us, is coming on the son of the wind . . . but what will he fight with? What weapon can kill the Enchanter?"

Her strange, sad cry changed to a voice of prophecy. "Because your children have been brave and adventurous, and have dared your displeasure to free me, I can tell you this. The only sword which can kill the Enchanter is one which combines the ice of the moon with the fire of the sun, the cold bite of steel, the warm strength of the growing earth."

"I will not be hustled," protested Lord John, his face still ominously dark. "*I* am the master smith here, and well able to champion the Four Families with such a sword. I am trained in all kinds of combat—" His voice, harsh and loud though it was, trailed away as Swanilda sadly shook her head.

"Even now, you do not understand," she murmured. "The children know. Ask them, while I call. They know why Adler Windhover must champion us all.'' Back she turned to the window, and, unwillingly, the adults had to look enquiringly at their children.

Jasper explained, tactfully keeping all hint of ''I told you so'' out of his voice, and repeating what Scruffy had told them, back in the caves. When he had finished, the adults looked grim, but their anger was no longer directed at the children.

''To sum up, Doppel and Lord Adler are almost one and the same person?'' asked Old Sol.

Jasper nodded.

''And to become a single entity again, Lord Adler must kill the Enchanter with a sword of Power,'' mused Lord John.

The children all nodded this time. ''*Only* Lord Adler can do it,'' said Jasper.

Slowly the adult members of the Four Families met each other's gaze. Finally, Old Sol chuckled ruefully. ''So—the crisis is upon us, whether we will or no. Where our children show the way, this time, we must follow, and not be far behind. Let us go to work.''

13

Fight to the Death

✿

Once convinced that Lord Adler was the one man who could kill the Enchanter, the heads of the Four Families were not backward in making their contribution to the coming fight.

Swanilda told them that she and the Eggchild had had to call Lord Adler and Argamath from beyond Quarrine, and that it would take several hours for them to fly the distance to Mootmeet. She was strained and distant in her manner, as if her whole being were absorbed in the Eggchild, and the song it was singing to draw its father to a battle which could be fatal for more than himself. She seemed unable to talk about herself, as though the enchantment was only partly broken, and she still could not see the Shrimp. The poor little boy was heartbroken, and could not be consoled, so when they left to prepare a weapon for Lord Adler, the adults took him with them.

The Shrimp, therefore, was the only one of the children to see the sharing of Power between the adults. They made no grand announcements to each other of what they *could* do if they wished.

They just did it, on the sensible assumption that they were all Powerful people. Princess Diana and Old Sol linked hands, and stood facing each other. Around them grew globes of silver and of gold light, and where the gold and silver merged, a bar of something solid came into being. Across the bar of pure ice and fire, Lord John, Lady Amethyst and Lady Fenella linked hands. Into the bar, Lord John poured all his knowledge of mining and smithying, so that the bar took shape and became a sword, to whose qualities he added the strength of steel, and the two women the endurance of all growing things which fight to live.

Finally, upon their ten linked, crossed hands rested a perfect weapon, which shimmered with its own life-glow. Together, they moved sideways to the prepared cooling trough, and Lord John said kindly, "Let the Shrimp's contribution be the water to temper the metal."

Together, they dropped their hands. The sword plummeted into the trough and a bolt of lightning crackled upwards where it hit the water.

Lord John reached under the surface, and drew out the beautiful, deadly weapon. His face was grim.

"So, a fit sword to fight the Enchanter," he said, and added, "Let us leave it in the Great Council Chamber, until it's needed. I'll give orders for watch to be kept for the arrival of Lord Adler, and the son of the wind."

"You believe Lady Swanilda and the Eggchild can call him?" asked Princess Diana.

"Don't you feel her Power?" demanded Old Sol, beard bristling with energy. "I certainly do, though at the moment there seems to be something missing."

"I agree," said Lady Fenella. "She's incomplete without her husband. I recognize it well."

Lord John touched her hand fleetingly, knowing how she missed her own husband.

"Come, then," he rallied them. "Let's go and make ourselves ready."

By mid-afternoon, everyone was anxious. The children were still up in the nursery wing with the Eggchild and Swanilda, who stood at the playroom window, staring far away over the forests in the direction of Quarrine.

Jasper knocked on the girls' bedroom door, and walked in to find Selena comforting a disconsolate Rosemary.

"What's the matter?" he asked, sitting down on the end of Selena's bed.

Rosemary's chin wobbled, and she said in a very small voice, "Lots of things."

"Like?"

"I want not to feel cross with our parents. I want Lord Adler and his family to be free to stay. But . . . but most of all, I want to know what it is the Eggchild's singing about. I've listened and *listened,* and I'm sure there're words. It's just that I don't understand them, but if I did, everything we don't know would come untangled!"

"My!" said Jasper, grinning affectionately at her. "You do want a lot, don't you?"

Rosemary gave a watery grin, and followed Selena and Jasper out to the playroom.

They were just in time to hear a loud "Halloo," followed by a blast on the guest-horn still hanging outside the great gates to Mootmeet. Someone, at least, had decided to talk.

"Who is it?" asked Rosemary, who wasn't tall enough to see out of the high windows.

"Doppel," called Selena and Zonn, and rushed to the door. Last out, Rosemary followed the other children along the corridors and up the winding stairways of Mootmeet to the platform on the walls above the great gates.

By the time they arrived, there was a crowd of

jostling servants filling the courtyard, while above them on the platform stood Lord John and Lady Amethyst, Lady Fenella, Old Sol and Princess Diana. All of them, noted their irreverent children, had taken great pains with their appearance. Old Sol was resplendent in a robe of gold cloth which fell to his knees. His long beard licked about his face like flames, and his mane of red hair looked burnished. He contrasted vividly with the cool cloth of silver worn by Princess Diana. Her knee-length silvery hair was bound about her brows by the crescent moon diadem which she rarely wore, and she held herself tall and still. The three other adults were no less gorgeously clad, Lord John wearing his favourite dark blue, his wife in purple, and Lady Fenella in the muted greens of her beloved growing things. Altogether they made a most impressive sight.

"Who comes to the gates of Mootmeet to sound the *guest*-horn?" asked Old Sol, with heavy sarcasm.

Doppel stared up, and replied courteously enough, "I would have come as a guest if I could."

"Oh, the time for pretence is past!" snapped Lord John. "What do you want with us?"

"Redress of my grievances."

"State them, and then maybe we'll state a few of our own."

"You have the Egg that sings. It is mine."

"It is *not* yours," stated Old Sol fierily. "It is with its mother."

Doppel looked a little taken aback, as though he had not bargained for this, but he had no chance to say any more. The watchman in the tower gave a shout, and pointed at a speck in the sky, which rapidly grew in size.

"Lord Adler and Argamath," whispered Rosemary to Jasper beside her, then turned to look

where he was staring, not up and out, but down
below into the courtyard.

The great gates were opening, and out below the
platform walked Swanilda with the Eggchild,
which sang and sang. The Raiders moved slowly
into a huge circle, with Doppel at its centre, then
stood, motionless and silent.

Like an arrow, Argamath dropped from the
sky, its huge wings winnowing, until it landed in
the courtyard.

"Quick, Jasper, run and fetch the sword!"
ordered Lord John.

The boy sprinted off towards the Council
Chamber.

Drawing his sword as he ran, Lord Adler hurried out under the arch of the gates to meet his
enemy. He gave no sign of seeing Lady Swanilda,
or the Eggchild. His eyes were fixed on Doppel.

"Hurry, Jasper, hurry, son," muttered Lord
John to himself as he stared downward at the circle below the mansion walls.

"So, you've come at last," sneered Doppel.
"Going to try your luck again? This time, I'll
finish you, Adler Windhover, and this whole
country shall be mine. I'll squeeze the people dry
for having opposed me so long."

"Save your breath, Doppel," said Lord Adler
coldly. "What do I care for this country? Maybe I
did once—I don't know, because *you* stole my
identity and my memory. If I hadn't been deliberately misled by the Sard boy, I'd have fought you
again before now."

Doppel's face was strained, but it was as nothing to the ghastly pallor and exhaustion of Lord
Adler. The children all knew he had been very ill,
and he looked it still, leaning on his sword. Rosemary took one look at him and almost gave up

hope. He should be in bed recovering on a diet of meat broth and herbs, not fighting for more than his life in the afternoon of a chilly autumnal day.

Jasper, running down the steps from the Council Chamber, opened his mouth to shout to Lord Adler to wait and take the weapon they had made, but it was too late. Rosemary felt cold and sick as her green gaze fastened on him, and she willed him to be skilful and quick. She willed him well and strong as he jumped back before a vicious slash from Doppel's sword.

Lord Adler moved straight from defence to attack, shifting his weight and balance to lunge forward straight for Doppel's chest. Doppel threw himself to one side, so that Lord Adler's blade sliced along his arm, leaving a red, dripping trail behind it.

Doppel did not even blink. He seemed totally unaware of the wound, and kept his whole concentration fixed on his opponent's eyes and sword. Rosemary realized that he was a first-class swordsman. She had heard Jasper telling her brother, a long time ago during a swordstroke lesson, that the sign of a good fighter was to watch the eyes of the opponent, not necessarily his weapon.

"You see any move that's going to be made in the eyes first," Jasper had said to Corrie. "Watch his eyes, and you've a good chance of beating him."

Rosemary fervently hoped this wasn't always true. Lord Adler looked so tired, and his movements were slowing. Doppel saw this too, and stepped up his attack. For a few moments, the din of steel on steel from the hollow was deafening. The flurry of swirling clothes and swiftly moving limbs made it difficult for the watchers to be clear about what was going on. The men struggled chest to chest for a long moment, each trying to break the hold of the other, and unbalance his opponent. Finally, Doppel pushed Lord Adler backwards, muttering an incantation, and followed up with a sweeping, unstoppable blow at his head. If the stroke had landed, it would have decapitated Lord Adler, but he dropped neatly to one knee, and the other man's weapon passed harmlessly above with a thin, keening sound.

"Now, now!" muttered Zonn. "One lunge and you've got him!"

"Ohh," wailed Selena, uncharacteristically. Rosemary was speechless. Lord Adler was looking disbelievingly and despairingly at the stump of his sword. The blade had fractured neatly at the base of the hilt, leaving him defenceless.

Doppel's face stretched and twisted in a mask of sheer animal triumph.

Jasper's arm swung up, and the Power-wrought sword flashed through the air, and landed quivering upright beside Lord Adler. Doppel's arm had swept back, muscles tense, for the short lunge which would transfix his helpless opponent.

The sword flashed forward, with all Doppel's weight behind it; then everything seemed to slow down so that each detail was clear.

Lord Adler raised his head as if to meet death squarely. Then the sword beside him seemed to leap into his hand, crackling with energy. Blinded, but still in mid-sweep, Doppel had no chance whatsoever to recover his balance. The sheer force of his missed blow had toppled him, and he fell straight on to the blazing sword. The blade transfixed him, freezing his blood, burning his heart and brain, piercing his ambition with the hardness of steel, and telling him how much he had misunderstood the warmth and Power of those he had sought to overthrow. He lay still.

Lord Adler swayed, then straightened wearily, and looked up at the sky.

"I am— I'm Adler Windhover!" he exclaimed, then, even more gladly, "My wings!" And suddenly, a shrill screaming filled the air: the triumphant sound of a bird of prey after a successful strike. Adler Windhover disappeared, and a great golden eagle spiralled into the sky, so swiftly that it was soon lost to sight. Only a shimmering sword, a crumpled figure, and the statue-like Night Raiders were left.

The arena below seemed somehow bereft, and Rosemary shuddered as she glanced at the still figure lying below her. But the Eggchild and the Shrimp equally claimed her attention: the Shrimp, because he was sick from sheer excitement, and the Eggchild because its lusty singing suddenly changed to a calling, calling, heart-breaking in its longing.

A speck reappeared in the sky, and plummeted earthwards. The eagle landed on the grass with talons outspread, and the shrill squeaking of the wind through its feathers as it braked drowned the song for a moment; then there was quiet, and the calm, sombre man they had known as Hawk knelt beside the Eggchild, which now lay on the grass by itself. His hands reached out to it, but the Shrimp had darted down from the platform and out through the gate, and flung himself between Adler Windhover and the Eggchild.

"Let it alone. It's *my* baby!" he yelled, and stamped his foot. Lord Adler sat back on his heels, so that he was on a level with the little boy, and said gently, "Yes, it is your baby, Shrimp. But *you* are *my* baby. Don't you remember?"

With a vaguely affronted look on his face, the Shrimp stared at the man in front of him. "I am not a baby!" he insisted.

"No, but when I last saw you, you were very little. You're four years old now, but when I last saw you, you were not quite three."

The Shrimp's eyes clouded, and he said, "It was cold, then."

"You're right. We were all out together, weren't we, visiting the ice-caves and the dragons. There was you, and I, and the Eggchild . . ."

"And Mamma," finished the Shrimp flatly. "An' nasty man came and you got angry."

"I was *very* angry, Shrimp. The 'nasty man' wanted to steal my dragons, and make them fight in a war, but I wouldn't let him. I didn't realize he was an Enchanter. I just didn't realize . . ." he muttered to himself, not looking at anything now. His eyes were blank, as though he were reliving that experience.

"Mamma turned the nasty man into a beetle," said the Shrimp challengingly, looking slyly at Lord Adler through his sandy eyelashes.

"Yes, of course she did," agreed the man, without the faintest flicker of disbelief, and all at once the Shrimp flung himself into his father's arms, laughing and crying at the same time.

"You *must* be my Daddy. You didn't laugh, but I felt your feathers go tickly, just like they used to! Do *you* love me?"

Adler Windhover held his son as though he'd never let go again, and rocked him to and fro comfortingly. Then he said, "But why do you ask whether I love you? Your mother and I both loved you, and—"

"No," said the Shrimp flatly. "Mamma doesn't love me any more!"

Suddenly, Adler Windhover seemed to grasp the sense of what his son was saying.

"Shrimp! Do you mean that Mamma is *here*?"

"Yes, but she can't *see* me," sobbed the

Shrimp. Lord Adler wheeled round to face the battlements.

"Swanilda!" he shouted. "Swanilda, come. You must have called me from afar, now you must come to me. Where are you?"

There was a gasp from the crowd as a great shining white bird swept down from the battlements, long neck outstretched for flight. It passed over the heads of Lord Adler and the Shrimp, as though heading for the wilderness; but as it skimmed over the transfixed huddle of the Enchanter's body, its wings seemed to crumple, and it fluttered to the ground.

Thinking only to help, Rosemary and Jasper ran down from the platform to pick up the Eggchild, while Lord Adler rushed to the struggling swan, whose wings beat heavily against the grass as it tried to lift itself into the air again.

He avoided its stabbing beak, and flung his arms round its body.

"Swanilda!" he cried. "Double enchantments *can* be broken; and I *will* break it. 'Nilda, come back!"

At once the thrashing stopped, and the beautiful woman fell forward into her husband's arms, her body doubled up in pain, and her face pearled with sweat.

"The baby!" she gasped. "Listen to the baby!"

Lord Adler turned to where Rosemary had crouched down, weeping bitterly, beside the Eggchild. She had been unable to hold it when she tried to pick it up. Its shell had been burning hot, but now it lay dull and cold on the grass. It looked dead. The light had gone from its many-faceted, glowing shell, and everyone saw with horror that it was split from end to end.

"It's broken!" wailed the Shrimp; but, as many eyes watched, the Eggchild's song began again. It was sweet and clear as always, but they could at last understand the words.

> *Of all children, I was foretold*
> *As the birdlike Egg, the Child of gold.*
> *And of all children, I am the child*
> *Who has control over all things wild.*

> *When men turn to savage ways*
> *Forgetting happier human days*
> *They become like beasts, and cease to be men,*
> *And all must come to the Eggchild then . . .*

> *Happy be folk on sea and land*
> *Who do not answer to my command,*
> *For they are human, not beasts at all.*
> *It is only beasts who must answer my call.*

As the song ended, the opaque, brownish casing of the Eggchild split into two neat halves, and fell away to reveal the sturdy kicking feet and waving arms of a perfect baby girl.

"Oh," breathed Rosemary, "I knew I'd understand if I could hear the song properly. The Raiders had to come when the Eggchild called them, because they'd turned into wild animals inside, and now they can't move until it releases them."

Lord Adler nodded, but it was his wife who spoke. Her voice was still faint with pain and weariness, but it gained strength as she spoke.

"When Ilkar Yumal came to our valley, he did not expect to find the great dragons guarded. That was one shock. His worst one came, though, when he realized that Adler's and my second child was that very rare thing in our Family, a child who could control every animal ever created, including humans who behaved like beasts. He knew that if the Eggchild ever hatched, he would have to obey it, because he was a man-beast himself."

She paused to catch her breath, and Rosemary went on, wonderingly, "But of course, he couldn't destroy it, because you and Lord Adler had protected it, even though doing that left you open to attack."

Swanilda nodded. "When I saw that Adler had been beaten, I used the last of my Power to compel him to take Argamath, and carry the Eggchild away with him. As long as any Power was left to him, Adler had to protect the Eggchild, even while he lay under enchantment, but when Power was almost gone from him, if that ever happened, he was to leave the Child in a place of safety."

"Our stable loft!" exclaimed Rosemary.

"So I *did* hear wings, that night!" added Jasper, and Adler Windhover agreed.

"Having had such battles fought over it, the Eggchild could only hatch when the Enchanter was overthrown," said Lady Swanilda softly. "She is fully born now, Rosemary. Pick her up, gently. She'll know it's you who's looked after her for so long. She'll tell you her name, and after that she'll be like any other normal baby."

Rosemary knelt again, and carefully picked up the Eggchild. She bent her head to listen. Everybody else heard only a soft fluting note, but Rosemary looked up happily and said, "Meet Melina, everybody."

"Welcome, Melina," came a chorus of voices, and Rosemary held the baby out to its mother; but Swanilda shook her head, and said, "Keep her, just a moment more, Rosemary. I've got another baby somewhere, and I've been missing him rather a lot."

All the adults had come down from the platform by now, so Swanilda moved gracefully away from her husband, and looked over at the Shrimp, who was peering in a lost and anxious way from behind Lady Amethyst's skirts.

"Aren't you going to say hello?" asked Swanilda, and held her arms out, fingers spread. The Shrimp's nose twitched as her fingers moved, and suddenly, he crowed with laughter, and spluttered.

> *Tickly feathers make you sneeze*
> *Fluttering downy in the breeze . . .*

But the rest of the rhyme was smothered as he launched himself at his mother and burrowed his way into her embrace.

"A bathtime nursery rhyme," explained Swanilda to the others, when the Shrimp had calmed down a bit.

"I wouldn't have thought bathtime posed any problems with the Shrimp!" murmured Rosemary, thinking of the times it had proved difficult to get the Shrimp *out* of water.

"Oho!" laughed Swanilda. "I can see you haven't tried getting him to use soap!" And there was a general laugh as the Shrimp pricked up his ears and said, "Soap?" on a squeak of alarm, and bolted for the refuge of his father.

"Why couldn't you see your son before, Lady Swanilda?" asked Lady Amethyst. "He's been doubly forlorn since the children broke the enchantment and brought you back to your true form."

"Oh! Please don't say that," exclaimed Swanilda in distress. She turned to her husband. "*You* tell them, Adler."

"The enchantment was double," explained Lord Adler sadly. "When Swanilda saw that Doppel was going to beat us, she used the last of her Power to compel me to protect the Eggchild. That made her completely defenceless against the Enchanter, and he was able to use her own spells against her. She had protected the Eggchild, so he hoped to enchant her in such a way that, to obtain her release, she'd have to gather together the two people she had protected—the Eggchild and me.''

"I think I understand," nodded Lord John. "The Eggchild was the only Power object which could break the first enchantment, and bring Lady Swanilda back to her own form. And you, Lord Adler, were the only one who could stop your wife becoming a Swan forever when the first enchantment was broken."

"Quite right, my Lord," nodded Lord Adler. "Whether she knew it or not, when the first enchantment was broken, she would still be only half in the world of normal life, and nothing would matter beyond calling me to her, wherever I was."

"Do you mean," demanded Princess Diana, "that Doppel intended to keep watch on where your wife was all the time? Then, even if he failed to capture the Eggchild and the enchantment was broken by someone else, he would still be on hand to destroy all of you together?"

Lord Adler nodded again, adding, "As it turned out, he failed to recognize your Family Powers for what they are, and so I now have *my* family together once more."

The Windhover family was invited into Moot-meet, and tactfully left alone until evening. The older children spent their time grooming and petting Argamath, who had stood patiently in the courtyard throughout the excitement. The adults dealt with the Night Raiders. Lord John ordered his guardsmen to take them far into the western mountains, and leave them there with plenty of food and some blankets. Princess Diana would then make them forget everything that had ever happened to them in the Country of the Four

Families. All they would remember were their names, and where they had come from originally. Any time they tried to turn east again, towards Quarrine or Argentia, they would become terror-stricken, which would make sure that they moved steadily away.

Princess Diana and Old Sol between them took care of the Black Ships. A terrifying storm would keep the ships moving westward for days, said Princess Diana vengefully, "and I don't care how many get wrecked along the way!"

The Raiders and the ships having been dealt with, the adults turned next to the thorny problem of the Windhover family, so Lord Adler and Lady Swanilda were invited down for discussions.

The children were left in the playroom, doing the extra work they'd been set as punishment for disobedience, and thinking wistfully how much they had enjoyed being together at Mootmeet. They had even enjoyed studying together, with Mr. Longthorn. Whatever decisions were made downstairs, they knew that soon now they would be going their separate ways again. For Rosemary, the only lightening of the gloom was that she'd soon be back with Corrie.

At last, however, they heard the doors of the Great Council Chamber crash as they were flung open.

"My father!" chuckled Jasper, then was as quiet as the others, to listen. Soon, they could hear footsteps approaching down the corridor, and Melina crooned to herself. The door opened.

"We've come to tell you what's been decided," announced Old Sol, rubbing his brown hands together happily. "We think it will suit every-body."

Adler Windhover smiled at his wife, who nodded back as she picked up Melina, and he said,

"We agree, sir. Now I have my family back, it will suit me well to have part of this great house to be our home. I'm glad that you will give us such a generous welcome."

Lord John Sard looked slightly uncomfortable. "We should not have been so welcoming, my Lord, if we had not heard, both from our children and from you, that Ilkar Yumal did not attack you first because he knew you to be greatest in Power, but because you opposed his use of your dragons in war. In this Country, there is no room for anyone greater than another. Our Power is truly shared. But now it will be divided five ways instead of four."

"We'll patrol the whole country, and do whatever is needed to help with wild life or domestic animals," promised Lord Adler.

"There is something more," said Princess Diana. She opened the book of Council Records she was carrying, and read: "Mootmeet will remain open and staffed all the year round. Mr. Longthorn will teach the children of the Five Families for three months at a time, after which they'll come home and plague us for the next three months."

"That's the first bit of humour I've heard of in Council Records!" exclaimed Jasper. Zonn slapped him on the back, while Rosemary and Selena hugged each other and their parents looked on with indulgent smiles.

"And long may the story of these four brave children be remembered," added Adler Windhover. He smiled at Rosemary, who would always be his favourite; then he took his tiny daughter from Swanilda, and cradled her in his arms. His tawny head bent over her, and he said in his deep voice, "As a family, we've waited long enough for peace, haven't we, Melina? We've fought for it, with your mother's life and freedom and mine at stake—your life, too. Now, we've earned our peace.

"Bless you, little Eggchild."

MURDER, MAYHEM, SKULDUGGERY...
AND A CAST OF CHARACTERS YOU'LL NEVER FORGET!

THIEVES' WORLD ™

EDITED BY
ROBERT LYNN ASPRIN and LYNN ABBEY

. . . .

FANTASTICAL ADVENTURES

One Thumb, the crooked bartender at the Vulgar Unicorn...*Enas Yorl,* magician and shape changer ...*Jubal,* ex-gladiator and crime lord...*Lythande the Star-browed,* master swordsman and would-be wizard...these are just a few of the players you will meet in a mystical place called Sanctuary. ™ This is *Thieves' World.* Enter with care.